Second

is

Best

BY

Aileen Friedman

ISBN – 13   978-062-059756-2

Website
http://aileenfriedman.co.za

Facebook
https://www.facebook.com/groups/353447231333743/

Twitter
@aileenlf

Editor
Franziska Annas
franziska.annas@gmail.com

Contribution
Tamara De Jager
tnsdejager@gmail.com

Cover Photos
Top photo
Baggies – Warner Beach
Georg PN Fourie
Georgpnf1@gmail.com

Bottom Photo
Doggy Beach – Gordons Bay
Cara Friedman
ifriedaman@gmail.com

Train Photo
Internet Archives

Cover Design
Cara Friedman
ifriedaman@gmail.com

Thank you, Lord Jesus,
for your love and mercy
and for blessing me
with my family whom I love so much.
I am truly blessed.

Phil 4:13 'I can do all things through Christ who strengthens me.'

Special thanks to
Linda Jones
for her never-ending support
and friendship.
You mean so much to me.

Table of Contents

Chapter one

Heavy raindrops pelted against the windows of the coffee shop forcing me to stare through the grey haze towards the ocean. Trees were bent over backward, resisting the force of the wind, and the waves of the sea seemed to argue with the sand, smashing against the shoreline in an angry and wild dance.

The storm violently ravaged the usually peaceful beachfront at Addington Beach, as people tried with all their might to remain upright as they ran – or attempted to run – for shelter. At the same time, everyone had to avoid debris flying around as the wind whipped it up and flung it around against its will. Umbrellas were of no use, they bent and buckled under the pressure of the wind, leaving their owners without cover from the drenching rain.

My mood was as grey as the weather outside and as black as the coffee steaming in my cup, and I felt as confused as the swirling waters lashing the beach.

Every few minutes the door to the coffee shop would swing open, and a bitterly cold draught would force its way in as the shop became more crowded with people desperately taking refuge indoors and warming themselves with a hot beverage. Quickly and easily they chatted and seemed to make friends. Yet, surrounded by the hustle and bustle I felt lost among them. I felt alone, afraid, and saddened beyond belief, without a friend in the world, and with no one who cared about whether I lived or died.

'May I sit with you at the table, please?'

I was lost in thought as I heard, 'Ma'am, excuse me, ma'am, sorry to disturb you…'

My stare got diverted when an elderly gentleman eventually tapped my shoulder to get my attention. I nodded without expression and returned to the intoxicating visuals outside, my coffee untouched.

'It sure is a crazy day today, where did this weather come from, eh?'

Ignoring him was my only reply, and he seemed to get the message, leaving me to my solitude among the drone and hum of the now over-crowded room.

To add a touch of drama to the already wild and untamed storm lightning decided to make an appearance – dancing across the sky and piercing through the heavy and monstrous clouds in zigzag flashes, swooping down to the ocean. At times, it felt as though it stung the windows right in front of my face and I flinched. With every ominous clap, it flung at the earth, the sheltering people around me shook and took a step back from the windows, seemingly fearful of its majestic power.

As the storm grew in ferocity so, my mood became, even more, downcast.

The lights flickered and from some resistance on their part, remained on, much to the delight of the patrons in the shop.

'Looks like the power is going to go out too,' said another elderly gentleman as he squashed himself into the seat next to my first guest.

I wondered who might fill the last seat at the table, but only for an instant as my thoughts and gaze remained fixated on the storm outside.

'May I join you?'

A woman about the same age as the men asked as she sat down in the vacant chair. The two gentlemen stood up until she was seated then plonked themselves back in their seats introducing themselves to one another at the same time. Hesitantly they looked at me inviting me to play in their game, but I very rudely offered them my shoulder and the back of my head.

In the background, the muffled sounds of chatter and teaspoons clinking against the china cups increased in volume. The coffee shop began to get stuffy and very warm due to the number of people seeking relief within its walls. Everyone took off their coats and scarves and made themselves more than comfortable, some even sitting on the floor, satisfied to remain there to wait out the storm.

I could barely see the ocean now – the grey haze from earlier had become a dark, almost black fog, but still, the wildness of the sea was inviting to me. I wondered how long it would take for the swirling waters to overcome me if I did not resist. I agonized over whether I was brave enough to attempt such an act.

Someone burst out laughing in a loud cackle and distracted my sordid thoughts, much to my annoyance. And then I shuddered at the realization of what I was contemplating doing.

Where had my life gone so wrong?

Chapter Two

Fred and Mildred (Milly) Raines, my parents, lived modestly and had been content and happy in their early years of married bliss. I was born, and they cherished their darling daughter, promising to raise me by His love and His will before God and the witnesses that were present. We were the truest example of the modern day happy family, with a house and the white picket fence and family dog – all serving God. I thought I would be the happiest child that had ever lived. I was what they had always dreamed of, and hence, I never had a sibling – as much as I would have loved one, especially when things went horribly south.

I was eleven and arrived home from school one day after eagerly jumping off the school bus while waving a quick goodbye to my friend Rachel. I was so eager to tell my mother my news that I didn't even notice the cars parked on the sidewalk in front of the house. Rushing up the path lined with the brightest marigolds in the street, I burst through the front door to tell my mother the excellent grade I had achieved on my spelling test.

'Mommy! You will never guess what I got for my spelling test! You will never, never, never guess! Momm…..' I yelled loudly, my voice echoing strangely.

I suddenly stopped mid-sentence when I noticed my mother sitting on the couch with red and wet eyes. To my astonishment, as he was normally at work during the day, my father was sitting next to her holding her hands, his head bent.

He straightened when he saw me, stood up and walked toward me, brushing past my aunt and uncle and other family members and friends that I suddenly noticed were also in the room.

'Kaye sweetie, something has happened, something not happy,' he said.

He came across to me and picked me up – he was a very big and strong man – and he carried me to where my mother was sitting. He sat down next to her while still holding me and finally rested me on his lap. My mother looked at me with tears streaming down her face, her lips quivering as my father spoke gently to me.

'Sweetie, do you remember how we spoke about grandpa not being very healthy?'

I nodded my head cautiously, remembering.

'Well,' my father went on, 'he had a heart attack this morning, and he has gone to be with grandma in Heaven.'

He stopped choking down his emotions, and a sob escaped his chest.

'Grandpa's dead?' I muttered as I began to cry, coming to the realization that my favorite man in the world, after my father, of course, will never speak to me again..

It had not been long, two years in fact, since my grandmother had died and so the emotions of that traumatic time were still very fresh in my mind.

My mother reached out and hugged me crying all the while. I knew her parents were now both in Heaven, and she had loved them very much.

From the death of my beloved grandfather, my mother inherited a lot of money, and it was that day that the slow decline of my modern day happy family began.

The first thing my parents did was to each buy a brand-new car. Then new furniture for the entire house and then I suddenly had a wardrobe any little girl would dream to have.

Then came the exotic holidays. My father would take his annual leave, and we would go somewhere exciting and where the sun was always blazingly hot. And for the rest of the year, they would go away on weekends and leave me with my aunt who got paid handsomely to take care of me. Let me not forget the parties that were held almost every other weekend – it seemed my parents had gained an increased number of new friends upon whom they could lavish their wealth.

One of their so-called new friends convinced my father to invest in a new business venture. He would then be able to safely leave his mundane job at the breweries – which he had kept even though they were wealthy, not wanting to use the inheritance to live off but rather to invest in something that would increase their wealth. Ideally, this would then allow my father to give up his job without depleting all the money – he very much wanted to work from home and in doing so be able to spend far more valuable quality time with his precious family. The opportunity was just far too appealing for him to pass up and precisely what he had been looking for to change his stance. To be able to go to his sweetheart daughter's swimming gala or her sports day and support her and cheer for her was a dream come true for him, the perfect father.

For months, my father's dream to be rich, work from home and have his loving and adoring daughter by his side almost all day every day got realized, and life was much more perfect than he or I could ever have imagined.

When I look back now and think of the turn of events, I realize I should have noticed the drinking slowly increasing from weekends and parties to every night. It started off with a glass of wine in a crystal glass, with dinner served on our new porcelain plates rimmed with gold. From one glass of wine, it progressed to wine all night until bedtime. Then eventually to the point where I would come home from school and find glasses, that had been filled with all kinds of alcohol all over the house; even though we had two full-time domestic maids to clean up and run around after my parents and the new air of wealth they carried upon their shoulders.

My father's new business partner came over to the house one evening, and I was sent to my room by my mother when the screaming from my dad's study drowned out the noise from the radio. I lay in bed with the bedroom door closed and the pillow over my head trying to drown out the sound of my father's voice. I had never heard him speak like that to anyone in my life – he always had the gentlest voice of any man I had ever met – and it made me so frightened that I cried in terror while I tried to drown out my tears with my sheets.

I heard my mother go into her bedroom and slam the door shut, to hide I presumed from the terrifying yelling. I wished she had come to me and held me and comforted me instead, but I lay there alone and wished that sleep would engulf me.

The front door banged shut shaking the adjoining windows. I heard the bottles in the kitchen rattle as my dad poured himself a large drink and, I assumed, gulped it down in one go as very soon the glasses were rattling again, and I heard him pour another, and another, and another.

Early the next morning I walked drowsily to the kitchen for breakfast. I was expecting to find a cheerful, loving husband and wife preparing coffee and breakfast before I went off to school. Instead, I found no one. Not even the maids were there. I thought perhaps after the previous evening's chaos they would probably just be a bit late, and so I opened the fridge to get out the milk, made myself some cereal and poured a glass of milk to drink. I sat down at the kitchen nook and started eating my cereal, still expecting my parents and the maids to walk in at any minute.

I put my cereal bowl and glass in the sink and then went to brush my teeth and wash my face in the bathroom. When I came out of the bathroom, I told myself I should go into my parents' bedroom to let them know I was getting ready to go to school and that they should get up too. As I was about to open their bedroom door, my mother came out, surprising me. I let out a little yelp and laughed, expecting her to find it funny too. Usually, this kind of thing would have us in stitches.

'Kaye darling, I have something to tell you, let's go to your bedroom.'

She put her arm around my shoulders and guided me towards my bedroom so that I sat on my large double bed and she sat softly down next to me.

Straightening her white satin gown around her waist and legs, she hesitated.

'Do you remember what happened here last night Kaye?'

I nodded, my eyes were big and round as she continued, 'Daddy was very angry because that man who pretended to be our friend lost all of our money. Daddy invested our money in a company, and that man used it to gamble with, and he lost it all. Do you understand what I'm saying, sweetheart?'

She stared at me pleadingly.

'Daddy must go back to work, and we have to sell all our nice things.'

'Yes, something like that darling.'

'Will Daddy still be at home so much? Because I like it when he is at home so much.'

'No dear, it will probably be like before grandpa died. Do you remember what that was like?'

'Yes, that was also okay.'

But it was never like that ever again. My father became increasingly depressed, rapidly becoming a shell of the man I had once known. He got a job at a local car manufacturing company with a good enough salary that we could live comfortably.

My mother took to drinking even more excessively during the day, and that led to endless arguments at night, and inevitably the arguing led to violence.

The cars got sold as was all the nice furniture and anything else my mother could get her hands on while I was at school.

During my last year at school, my father was put on short time at the car factory which meant that he was often at home during the day with my mother. All they did was drink themselves into a stupor.

Chapter Three

The sun baked down on the bonnet of Boyd's car, and I rested my arm against it, not thinking for a moment, and had to whip it away as I felt my skin burn. Boyd was one of only three boys in our senior year that was old enough to get his driver's license, of course, this made him popular – not that being popular interested him much. He was an average student, an average athlete and just wanted to get this final year over with.

No one in our class could believe that it was our senior year already, our final year. And we only had eight months to go. At times, it was too surreal to comprehend that in a couple months' time, we would all be going our separate ways after being in one another's lives since the first grade.

Boyd and his best friend York slowly walked towards the car. I could see they were deep in conversation, both staring at the ground as they draped their heavy bags loaded with books over their shoulders.

They let their bags fall with a thump to the ground on reaching the car, and Boyd put his arm around my shoulders and kissed me lightly on the forehead aware that a teacher would probably be watching. They found romances between students extremely entertaining, and we were careful to avoid any teasing.

The two boys climbed into the front of the car, and I slid onto the back tan leather seat. I could see their serious moods lifting as we headed to the perfect waves that waited for us at Baggies in Warner Beach.

As we did every day after school, we went to the beach before Boyd took me home. We all always kept a bag of spare clothes in Boyd's car for our afternoons on the beach.

While Boyd and York endlessly conquered the waves, I managed to stand on my surfboard a few times. Though I had been doing this for many years now, I had still not mastered the art of surfing.

I sat on the hot sand; a towel draped over my back and shoulders, protecting me from the glare of the sun – it was a particularly hot and humid day for May on the South Coast of

Natal, and I knew the discomfort in store for me if I got sun-burnt.

By three o'clock almost our entire senior year was at the beach and, as we did every day, we sat together and laughed and joked around with one another, discussed school-related topics and our plans for the future, not fully aware that life as we knew it would ultimately change. The small café at Baggies Beach made a fortune out of our healthy appetites and our terrible thirsts, this was always the happiest part of my day.

Boyd was always close by, his dark brown hair had smudges of blonde from the sun, and his sun-kissed skin and good build were enough to make me smile and swoon at any given moment. He had hard features that, if you did not know him very well, made him look angry, and yet behind those harsh features was a very caring and kind person, but he kept those feelings reserved only for the people very close to him, and of those, there weren't many.

Among all the different personalities that made up our class of '75, there always had to be one that was the clown, the one that you could rely on to entertain everyone else. And that someone was York. He had such a comical personality and found humor in everything. He was tall, tanned of course, with blonde sun-bleached hair of course and he wore glasses most of the time, which hid his lovely hazel eyes. They suited him, though, almost making him look even more handsome and more mature.

Somehow on this particular day, he had gotten hold of a piece of sponge that at a quick glance looked exactly like a piece of cheese. He stuck it into his sandwich camouflaging it a little with the lettuce, and as one of the boys came walking toward the café York offered the poor starving sucker a bite, and naturally, he took a huge mouthful. With everyone watching him he chewed for a second then realized that the piece of sponge half hanging out of his mouth was in fact not cheese, and he spat it to the ground cursing York. We were in fits of laughter. York, the clown, had conquered again.

As it was such a perfect day and since it was a Friday, we stayed on the beach until the sun had set, then went home to greet our families and then those of us that were fortunate enough to have easy-going parents, made our way back to the beach and remained there until sunrise. Obviously, this was not the norm on every weekend, but we did as children did and begged our parents for the favors, and if we managed to win them over then, we would experience the happiest fun-filled memories to carry in our hearts for the rest of our lives.

Boyd kissed me goodbye in the car as was our routine – it was always my decision not to have him walk me to the door – and I slowly got out of the car, waving and smiling goodbye.

'See you in two hours!' Boyd yelled out of the window as he drove off from the sidewalk.

I dragged my legs along the pathway lined with a few drooping flowers and grass that was growing between the paving stones. The grass in front of the house should have been mowed weeks ago, and I knew if I did not do it this weekend it would never get done. Fortunately, it was a relatively small garden.

As I turned the handle and pushed the door to open it, I was, as always, greeted by the unwelcome stench of alcohol and stale cigarettes. Holding my bag tightly over my shoulder to ensure it would not bang against any furniture, I headed for my room. First I tiptoed past my mother who was sprawled out on the couch, the last sip still waiting at the bottom of her whiskey glass, then past my father who was staring in a drunken stupor at the TV from his armchair. Same scene different day! Quietly I laid my bag on my bed and took out my school uniform and added it to the week-load of dirty laundry in my washing basket in the corner of my room.

I tried to make my room as pleasant as I possibly could, under the circumstances. I had a single bed covered with a bed linen set patterned with pink flowers on a light yellow background that had been given to me as a birthday present by Boyd's mother a year ago. I had a small table I used as a dressing table, and a mirror edged with flowers that my best friend Rachel had given me that same birthday. There were a few photos stuck on the wall of Boyd and me and all our friends enjoying crazy happy moments together. Against the wall opposite my bed stood a white wardrobe, small, but big enough for the few clothes I possessed – all bought with money I'd earned myself or else from money I'd saved from gifts on birthdays or at Christmas.

I exchanged the school books in my bag for clothes, and slipped into the bathroom to shower, still hoping I would not awaken my drunken parents.

When I stepped out of the shower and dressed in a pair of jeans and a light grey sweater, I thankfully still could not hear any movement from the living room.

Back in my room, I put on my sneakers and picked up the thick warm jacket belonging to Boyd but which I had claimed, then lifted my bag over my shoulder, silently clicked and locked my bedroom door and tiptoed back towards the living room. I found the note I had left my parents the previous Friday which simply read, *"Gone to a beach party, be home Sunday,"* and I lifted it off the kitchen counter and moved it to the dining room table. At least, if it were not in the same place, they probably wouldn't even notice it was the same letter. I knew they wouldn't realize it was the same letter since they had no concept of which day of the week it was or the time of day or possibly that I even existed half the time.

As silently as I had entered the house so I exited it and sat on the sidewalk until Boyd arrived and whisked me off to where I would be as happy as the rest of our friends.

On the beach, we made a huge bonfire after we had barbequed a few pieces of boerewors and made boerewors rolls. Music blared from the portable radio someone had brought along, and we listened to our favorite music on the late night station, to which we danced, our bare feet digging into the now cool sand.

York started a new game that we all took great delight in playing. We chased crabs as they came out of their little holes in the sand, as the sea water bubbled up to the surface. We never actually caught one, but it was just such immense fun to see who could get to one before it burrowed back into the sand – a silly game and yet we were highly entertained by it.

We eventually snuggled up in our sleeping bags next to our favorite persons and fell asleep to the sound of the ocean crashing on the sand as the swells broke. No matter how loud the sea sounded, it was always good therapy, like rocking a baby to sleep. I slept well that night, cuddled up to Boyd, and dreamed of floating away on a cloud.

Chapter Four

We sat in the assembly hall one normal school day morning, chatting with our peers and waiting for Mr. Layder, the school principal, to make his appearance. In a long black graduation cloak he looked like Batman from behind, and as he walked down the assembly hall aisle and up the stage steps, we all stifled giggles until he stood behind the podium.

We sat upstairs in the gallery and looked down from our senior pedestals at the rest of the school. We were seniors, and this was our last year of school.

Mr. Layder went through all the usual rituals of Bible readings, announcements, singing and then one more announcement that finally had all the seniors, especially the boys, in a deadly silence.

'All the Matric boys are to remain behind after assembly and to please gather together here in the front rows of the hall to receive your National Defence call-up papers.'

I shivered and looked at Boyd sitting on the boys' side of the hall; his face was solid; the call-up had finally arrived. It was enough to ruin all our plans for the future. One whole year of our lives would get put on hold.

After assembly, I sat in the registration class worrying over which call up Boyd would get. Would he go in January or in July?

Where would he be going?

Would he and York be going to the same place?

I hoped so.

I looked around the classroom, and except for a few girls chatting, we all sat in our seats pensively, wondering and worrying.

The bell rang, and I muttered my annoyance to Rachel that the boys had not yet finished in the hall, that meant that I would now only see Boyd at maths class, and we would hardly have a chance to talk in this class since Mr. Rotherford was so strict.

I waited outside the maths class as several others joined me from their respective classes. My heart pounded against my ribcage as I finally spotted Boyd and York walking towards me.

Boyd slumped against the wall next to me, his left shoulder almost over me, and he leaned his forehead on mine and sighed, shaking his head slightly.

'When?' I asked quietly, my heart in my throat.

He let out another sigh as he said, 'January,' and then another sigh escaped his lips.

I held his face in my hands and fought back the tears that wanted to pour from my eyes.

He pulled away from me at the sound of the classroom door opening and kids pushing and shoving their way past us.

'Talk more at lunch break,' he whispered as he kissed my ear and moved to stand with the rest of the boys on the other side of the classroom door.

I noticed the other boys were also solemn, their usually jolly attitudes subduedly forgotten. But then since they had all just received the same news, it was no wonder at all.

The only way anyone could be excused from their National Defence duty was if they were declared medically unfit. Which not one of these boys was, that was for sure. Or, of course, if they got accepted to university but then they had to fulfill their duty once they had completed their degrees. So either way, there was no escaping it.

Finally, at lunch break, I could get all the details. We sat under the huge rubber tree in the massive courtyard – strictly designated for the seniors only – at the back of the buildings between the school and the parking area.

'I'm going to Bloemfontein to the Infantry services,' Boyd said fiddling with my fingers as he spoke and held my hands.

We were aware the teachers would be watching as they always were, but our minds were too occupied with the current turn of events. I felt the teachers would be sympathetic to our case today, and they were. No one disturbed us.

'I'm going to Pretoria to the Technical Services, I think they call it "Tiffies,"' said York, who with no girlfriend did not really seem to mind going at all.

York stood up and went over to a group of boys all looking at one another's call-up papers and discussing their destinations descriptively with their hands.

'So you're going to college then in January, and when I get back, I'll join you there. It's just a year, and we'll be allowed home every few weeks, Kaye.'

Boyd lifted my chin and brought my eyes up to his, the truth in his eyes so real.

'I told you I cannot afford college.'

'I told you my parents said they would sponsor your tuition.'

'Your parents don't like me so why would they pay for my tuition? I still don't believe it.'

'They don't like your parents; it's not that they don't like you. We'll ask them tonight, and you can hear it from the horse's mouth, okay?'

He smiled at me, his harsh features warming instantly.

I smiled back and had no further chance to argue the point as all the other boys descended upon Boyd and his call-up papers.

Finally, school was done for the day, and as usual, we all headed to Baggies Beach. The conversation once again revolved around the call-ups, but was eventually exhausted of all possibilities and then the surf was up.

Claude and Verina Langford reclined on the sofa in their living room, their son Boyd and I perched in armchairs in front of them while they read the news.

Verina shook her head.

'I hate the laws of this country, using our children as their pawns.'

She began to cry, and Claude lovingly comforted her while Boyd just sat in his chair looking at the floor. I did not know what to do or say so I just stared at the floor, emulating Boyd.

'You will just have to go to university, and then you will be exempted,' Mrs. Langford said with a hint of hope in her voice.

'I will have to go when I finish with university nevertheless, and by then I will probably be the oldest person in my squadron. No thanks! I'd rather do it now and get it over and done with.'

Mr. Langford stood up and moved about the living room, seemingly pondering the issue and then after a little while he spoke.

'It might give you time to consider what you want to study and what career choice you should pursue. It's just a year and will give you a lot of time to think about the future.'

Holly, Boyd's ten-year-old sister, came into the living room from her bedroom and sat on Boyd's lap.

'You going to be a soldier?'

'I'm going to pretend to be a soldier just for a year,' he smiled at her.

'I like it when the soldiers march.'

Boyd hugged her, and Mrs. Langford burst into tears bordering on hysteria.

There were seven months left until January.

Chapter Five

I closed the front door leaving my mother typically slouched in a drunken stupor on the couch, and my father in the armchair in front of the TV with a glass in one hand and a cigarette in the other. Neither was even remotely aware of what day it was or that I had even walked past them twice already.

Outside the black entrance door of the house, I stood with my back against it, my heart heavy and sad. In every one of my school friends' houses right now, their mothers, after weeks of searching for the perfect dress for their perfect daughters, were helping their daughters climb into them. They had been with their daughters a few hours earlier at the hairdresser where the girls had magic done to their usual ponytails and had makeup applied that aged them in seconds.

And when finally they put on their shoes that stated their outfit "complete," their mothers would exclaim from sheer love and delight. I could just picture it. With their hands around their mouths, and covering their noses, they would then extend their arms out towards their daughters and embrace them, filling their hearts with even more love that they held for their daughters.

Not in my house!

The fathers would wait patiently in the living room with the nervous date, all the while staring at the boy from the corners of their eyes. The father would read the riot act to his daughter's date and threaten him if he dared mistreat his baby girl, lay a hand on her or not treat her with the respect she deserved.

The nervous date would simply reply, 'Yes sir,' for fear of saying anything that would make the father, even more, intimidating.

Not in my house!

And my heart ached.

I made my way down the path to the car in the driveway. My dress shoved in a bag; I had my vanity case and a tog bag with spare clothes in, under my arm, as I would be spending the night at Boyd's after the Matric Farewell dance. Mr. Langford was waiting in the car – it had just been washed and was sparkling – and once I had slid into the back clutching my dress and belongings he pulled off, and we made our way to their house.

'Kaye darling, you have got to hurry. If Boyd has to sit around any longer, he's going to chicken out and not wear the suit, and I will be so disappointed. Come, come, dear, let's get you dressed,' Mrs. Langford greeted me at the door and excitedly hurried me to the guest room where she had smelly oils burning and flowers in a vase on the dresser.

'The room looks so lovely, thank you, Mrs. Langford. I'm sorry if I have inconvenienced you in any way at all.'

'Nonsense dear, it is all my pleasure! Sit, let's get your hair done.'

And so I sat on the chair in front of the dresser while Boyd's mum fussed over my long blonde sun-bleached hair, twirling and twisting with a pair of tongs. About half an hour later I had twirls of blonde locks hanging about my face.

She put her hands on my shoulders and swiveled me around until I had my back to the mirror, and then she put her hand under my chin and lifted my head gently toward her, her long nails tickling my skin.

'Now for your makeup, look up at me, please.'

'Please don't put too much on, I never wear it, and it will irritate me before I even get to the dance I'm sure of it.'

'Silly dear, of course, I won't, now shoosh so that I can get done. Look up at me.'

She brushed my face with powder and pasted on cold liquid stuff. She added more powders to my eyelids and reshaped my eyebrows – that hurt a little – then she added the mascara to my flickering eyelashes. Every time she came near my eyes with the brush we both giggled madly, her soft peppermint breath blowing softly across my face all the while.

I turned and faced the dresser to see if I even recognized the girl in the mirror.

'No, you can't look yet! Not until you're finished dressing. Come this way and let's get this dress over your head without messing up your hair and makeup.'

Mrs. Langford pulled me up with her hands linked in mine and moved me toward the cupboard doors away from the mirror.

I let my gown fall to the floor feeling very embarrassed as I stood naked, except for my underwear in front of her. But she took absolutely no notice as she took the dress off the hanger and slid her arms through it from the bottom to the top, then she raised her hands over my head and plopped the dress down over me.

'Mind your hair and face as it comes over,' she said a few times and I took heed.

The dress was ruby satin, with a halter neck and a tightly fitted bodice and a four-paneled full-length skirt.

She then opened the shoe box and slipped the ruby stilettos onto my feet, completing my look.

She put her arms around my shoulders, turned me back to face the mirror and then stepped back clapping her hands in glee, thrilled with her achievement in manipulating this makeover.

I looked in the mirror and stared in total awe.

Was that truly me in the mirror?

My blonde hair that was in complete contrast to the ruby dress accentuated my green eyes; my round features looked soft and so grown-up. I had to take a really good look to make sure that was me in the mirror.

'You look beautiful. Now, come, let's go to the living room, I'm sure those men are sweating in anticipation.'

I suddenly grabbed Mrs. Langford's arm and stopped her from walking out the door.

'Mrs. Langford, thank you so much for everything. I wish I'd bought you a gift or something…' I trailed off.

She looked at me, and I'm sure I detected a tear in her blue eyes as she leaned forward and gently put her arms around me hugging me ever so lightly making sure not to mess up the dress, hair, and makeup.

'My dear, it has been a pleasure. It's going to be years before Holly has her dance and besides, I enjoyed doing it. You look like a princess my dear!'

She leaned forward and gently hugged me again.

Mrs. Langford walked ahead of me and announced to Mr. Langford and Boyd that I was ready. They both stood up instantly and faced the passageway that leads to the bedrooms. Boyd wrestled with his tuxedo trying to find a position he felt comfortable in, but before he got there, I made my grand entrance.

Boyd's face was a dream, his usually harsh features softened into a mesmerized gaze and his smile was so broad it took up most of his face.

A slap on the back from his father shook him back into the moment.

He walked towards me with his arms outstretched, and he took my hands in his.

'You look, you look, like, like a superstar, like a goddess. You look beautiful.'

He tried to say more but could not find the words. He didn't have to, what he had said was more than I needed to hear.

I beamed and felt like I was floating on such a high cloud from which I never wanted to climb off. Everything was so perfect, and at this very moment, I felt the way I knew every other girl in my senior year did, although I was in a different house. But for once it didn't matter, and I smiled.

Mr. Langford presented me with a single orchid that in his mesmerized state, Boyd had forgotten to give me.

'You do look truly lovely my dear,' he said as he handed it to me, his eyes shining.

We made our way to the school hall in Boyd's sparkling clean pumpkin of a car, a perfect beginning to an important part of any school girl's life.

Boyd in a suit, me with my dress, hair, and makeup, and combined with the fantasy decor themed school hall, the friendliness of all the teachers and the ambiance of being "grown-up," it all culminated into a magical evening and was the answer to any girl's Cinderella dreams.

Naturally, there was an after party, very much against the wishes of the school but it was held every year nevertheless. It goes without saying that ours took place on the beach.

We arrived after midnight, spent no time at all getting the fire going and the music blaring. We danced on the sand in our evening gowns, the boys in their suits, and the bright moonlight cascaded across the ocean and danced along with us in the movement of the waves. It was so romantic, granted we had all been drinking (some a little too much), but still, it was the most romantic evening I had ever had. Those that had to go home did, but for the rest of us, we stayed and allowed a magical moment in time to engulf us.

Chapter Six

Everyone mingled around, attaching themselves to their loved ones or standing close by, holding on to the last few valuable minutes available.

Mrs. Langford held Boyd around his waist as if she was glued to him, unfazed by the heat, and he held my hand tightly with his free hand. Mr. Langford stood close to his wife in support of her.

It was baking hot, and the humidity had surely reached a dangerous level. My body was wet with the clammy moisture in the air. The little tank top and hot pants I was wearing got stuck to my body like a second skin.

I noticed a lot of our school friends, slightly waving to each other as our eyes made contact – but only in acknowledgment, certainly not to show happiness at seeing them here, as this meant they were also sadly saying goodbye to someone they loved.

York finally arrived with his parents Layne and Aubrey Keller, and although his mother was not as clingy as Mrs. Langford, she stood her ground next to him trying very hard to hide her tears.

York seemed unperturbed about leaving – smiling and making jokes to ease the tension in our little circle, as usual. Neither his parents were impressed with his attitude.

I didn't know what to say to ease the tension I saw in Boyd's face, afraid that if I spoke, I would not be able to control the flood of despair, I felt at the imminent departure of these two very special boys.

A man in army attire stood at the camp entrance under the huge archway that had "Natal Command" written in huge letters around the arch, and then he blew a whistle.

Everyone went silent as he spoke into a megaphone. He called out the various destinations, and all those going there were instructed say their last goodbyes and make their way to the waiting trains.

'Oh no,' was all Mrs. Langford could say as she sobbed, setting off York's mum and me.

As she hugged Boyd tightly, he held her with one arm and still held onto me with his free hand as if he would never let me go.

Mr. Langford eventually pried her off Boyd so that he could say goodbye to his only son, and so that Holly too could say goodbye to her brother and so that he and I could have a few moments together.

'Wait for me please, don't forget me or find someone else Kaye, please?' he begged me as the tears trickled down his face, the fear of leaving now a reality.

He wrapped his arms around me and buried his face in my neck.

'I love you; I will be here waiting for you, I promise…' I choked away the hysteria I felt rising inside of me.

'Boyd, we've got to go,' York called him, ready to pull him away from our embrace if he needed to.

Slowly we let go of each other, our eyes bright with tears. York gave me a gentle, affectionate hug goodbye and promised to write to me. Boyd picked up his bag, and then the two of them walked through the gates of the camp, turning around only once to wave goodbye.

I thought my world would collapse right then.

Six weeks seemed like forever until I would see Boyd again.

Although Boyd and York were going to different camps, they were fortunate enough to be traveling on the same train. Thank goodness for small mercies.

I couldn't accept Boyd's parents' offer to pay for my college tuition. As kind and generous as it was, I did not want to indebt myself to anyone. Instead, I got a job at the local newspaper and decided to study journalism part-time. It would probably take me years to complete the degree, but in the end, it would be my achievement and of something I knew I would be proud.

Almost immediately after school, Rachel left to spend the next five years at Wits University in Johannesburg, and I was fortunate to find an apartment to share with a girl my age, Evelyn. She was studying full-time, and her parents owned the apartment which meant the rent was fairly reasonable.

I was just so grateful to get out of my parents' house. I sometimes wondered when I went to visit them if they were even aware that I did not live there anymore.

Every day after work I made a beeline for the post box in the foyer of the building, with the hope that there would be a letter from Boyd.

The days when my hopes came true, and there was a small white envelope with my name and address written in Boyd's handwriting, my heart would scream out loud with happiness. I felt something very similar the day I finally received a letter from York.

Boyd's letters were pretty much always the same. He would complain about how much he hated the army and the sergeants who did nothing but shout verbal abuse at them. How disgusting the food was and how much he missed me. Sometimes I could feel his hurting through the words written on the paper, and my heart would break for him.

Mrs. Langford phoned me one evening.

'Kaye dear, I got a letter from Boyd with the details of his six weeks' basics passing out parade. We are going to drive up and wanted to know if you'd like to come along. I'm very sure he will be just delighted if you do.'

'Oh thank you so much, gosh I definitely will go. Thank you!'

'It's in two weeks' time. I'll give you a ring you closer to the time with definite arrangements. Have you heard from him lately?'

'I received a letter three days ago; he seems so unhappy. I miss him so much.'

'Well, I don't blame him. If I had my way, he would never have gone in the first place. I will phone you again soon dear, bye for now.'

I smiled broadly, thrilled at the thought of seeing him in two weeks' time again. It seemed like an eternity since we had said goodbye.

'And that big smile?' Evelyn asked curiously.

'In two weeks I get to see Boyd. I'm going up to Bloemfontein with his parents.'

With that, I floated to bed happy.

Chapter Seven

The five-hour drive to Bloemfontein seemed to take forever even though I slept most of the way on the back seat of Mr. Langford's very smart Jaguar, and he did not drive slowly either. We checked in at a hotel close to the army base, and all I wanted to do was run there, find Boyd, hold him and never let him go. Being so close and not able to see him was driving me insane. I was restless and anxious at the same time.

In just a few hours I would see Boyd. I got dressed in a cool pink summer dress with flat white sandals and was ready at least an hour before we were to leave. I walked about the hotel room endlessly trying to hasten the time.

Poor Mr. Langford had to cope with both of us women in our anxious states and keep himself calm at the same time.

We arrived at the army base and parked as near to the huge main entrance building, made of red brick, three stories high as possible. We walked up the long paved pathway from the parking area between the walled gate and the large glass doors that led into the building. It was cool inside, and my skin relished the feeling. Glass cabinets displaying military memorabilia – totally uninteresting to me, filled the foyer of the main entrance hall. We went through the foyer and exited at the opposite side from which we had entered, stepping out onto the main parade ground. Behind the parade ground were the barracks, hundreds of them.

I wondered which one was Boyd's.

It was very warm already; I was sure that when it reached midday, it would be scorching. Finding sheltered seats with a decent view of the parade ground wasn't too difficult since we were of the first to arrive. I knew that from where I sat I would find Boyd among the other men all dressed in their fine step-outs.

The podium filled up with all the dignitaries and other not so important people. Once they got settled, the band came marching in, playing very well and doing all sorts of formations while playing and appreciating the applause from the audience.

Then the boys, or rather now, the men, came marching onto the parade ground from the right corner of the grounds. They marched past the dignitaries and then to the center of the field where they stopped and faced the podium, one squadron at a time. They marched with precision, with sharp and determined movements, their footsteps sounding like one giant's foot stomping the ground, their brown army step-out uniforms, without a single crease, moved in tune with their bodies.

I knew Boyd was in the E squadron, so when they finally made an appearance, I almost broke my neck trying to find him. And there he was! I was shocked to see how thin he was – he looked younger than a schoolboy. His face wore a grimace, and although he was keeping time with his marching, he looked so very much out of place. This man was such a far cry from the young surfer I'd said goodbye to six weeks ago.

The parade went on forever, and I was bored stiff listening to the endless speeches and watching the men march up and down, passing us occasionally but pointlessly. I kept my eyes on Boyd as much as I could and all the while he wore a face of unhappiness.

Finally, it was over, and we were allowed to visit with our loved ones.

Mrs. Langford, as elegant and as graceful as she always was, simply tossed it all aside when she saw her son. She squealed and ran and threw her arms around him, Mr. Langford, Holly and me right behind her. Boyd greeted his family with unbridled affection while I stood to one side waiting impatiently for my turn.

He took one step from them and flung his arms around me, almost squeezing the life out of me. I had my arms around his neck, pulling him to me, trying to capture his smell, his touch, his feel, all that for which I had longed.

'Kaye, I've missed you so much...' he mumbled into my ear and pulled me into his embrace, even closer if that were at all possible.

We were completely lost within each other, totally oblivious to the people around us hugging, greeting and talking to one another on the massive parade ground, as the clear midday sun baked down on us.

'Let me look at you,' I said finally, pushing myself away from him just a few centimeters to get a good look at his smooth and clean shaven face.

'I love you,' I said, staring into his eyes making sure he understood how I felt just in case he had forgotten.

'I love you so much,' he replied, touching my cheeks with his hands, gently and lovingly staring into my eyes, making sure I understood how he felt too.

'Let's get lunch,' Mr. Langford said with a smile, putting an arm around his son.

Boyd quickly rushed off and returned a few minutes later with his army bag stuffed with clothes for the weekend.

During lunch and for the rest of the afternoon we listened to his disgruntled feelings of basic training, the officers and even more so the awful food. What he seemed to enjoy the most was the shooting, having discovered he was something of a crack shot.

Who would've guessed this surfer boy with hardly any ambition or sporting talent would turn out to be a crack shot?

His parents eventually dragged themselves to bed, unable to keep their eyes open or their ears focused on hearing any more of Boyd's stories. Holly had long ago succumbed to the long, exciting day, and we were finally alone.

'I've been so terrified of getting a Dear John letter,' Boyd said while tucking a strand of hair behind my ear.

'Why would you think that? I told you I would wait for you – surely you should know how much I love you?' I held his face in the palms of my hands and kissed the tip of his nose.

'I love you, Boyd. I would never do that to you.'

He kissed me for the longest time, my spine crawling and my skin tingling in sheer delight. It felt like my heart stopped beating and my lungs ceased breathing, it felt as if every organ in my body shut down and savored his touch and all I wanted to do was disappear in his love.

For some time we just lay beside each other, relishing the closeness of our bodies, and I thought back to that night on the beach after we'd chased the crabs.

'I hate the army Kaye; I don't know how I am going to stick it out for a year. I absolutely hate it.'

I could immediately sense the frustration and exasperation he felt as he swallowed the thick tears back down his throat, and I wasn't sure what to say.

'Before you know it you'll be back home, and this will never have to happen again, and we can get on with our lives. Just hang in there, please. Just don't do anything stupid, please?'

'I won't, don't worry; it's just that I hate being here. The only thing I look forward to is your phone calls and your letters and when we go shooting.'

He yawned widely and slowly snuggled up to me on the couch so that we were both comfortable and eventually we were both fast asleep in each other's arms, dreaming sweetly for a change.

At the breakfast buffet in the hotel, Mrs. Langford continued her barrage of questioning, trying to convince herself that her son was doing well in the army. Boyd did not tell them how much he hated it – he knew his mother would probably become hysterical.

'Do you hear from York at all?' I asked while sipping down my freshly squeezed orange juice.

At that moment, a waiter dropped a glass that immediately got the attention of everyone in the very full restaurant. Embarrassed, he apologized and swiftly cleaned up the mess, and everyone continued to eat, drink and chat, the din that was briefly disturbed chimed once more.

'He writes quite often. He seems to be loving it. He says he's going to become a mechanic when he leaves the army since he's doing that kind of stuff at his base already.'

'Yes, he does seem to be happy. I've only had one letter from him, but from that letter, I could sense he was happy.'

After breakfast, we all went for a drive through the town and landed up at a zoo. Instinctively we decided to go in.

As we walked very slowly around the enormous zoo, looking at the variety of incredible creatures in their enclosures that were designed to be as close to the natural habitat the animal originally came from, we chatted, laughed and even got very serious at times.

It was a lovely day for Boyd. He was the center of attention and showered with love and affection by all of us. He walked around with his one arm linked to mine and the other into his mother's, not letting go for passers-by. Everyone had to maneuver around us, much to our amusement of course.

The hour when Boyd had to return to the base camp came much too quickly. Our hearts fell to our feet with a thump when he said goodbye again and walked into the gates of the camp just as he had done six weeks ago in Durban.

We all told him how much we loved him, at least, a hundred times, and he did the same in return. It was as if saying it just that once more would make it truer.

He held my hands in his against his heart. His face contorted with anguish.

'Don't leave me. I love you; please wait for me...' he pleaded as he kissed me one last time.

He put his arms around me and hugged me then turned around and walked back through the entrance doors, looking over his shoulder only once and waving briefly, before being swallowed up by the red brick walls.

Chapter Eight

Evelyn had gone to the coffee shop at her church like she did every Saturday, but for me, I lived for this phone call from Boyd.

In the last three months, he seemed to have become somewhat happier. The intense basic training and verbal abuse from the officers had mostly come to an end, and he had done so well with his shooting that they had moved him to that division. I wasn't sure what they called it; I knew he had told me several times, but I just couldn't or did not want to remember.

The phone rang, and I practically dived on it to answer it, so eager just to hear his voice.

'Hello, my sweet.'

His voice sent my heart pounding at those three simple words. I missed him so much.

'Hi, how are you?'

We exchange titbits about our week then he said, 'I got some news today.'

He went silent to prolong the anticipation.

'What Boyd? Tell me already.'

'We're going to the bush for a training exercise this week.'

'What?'

'Don't worry; it's not like going to fight for real. It's all set up like they do in the movies.'

'And you're happy to do this?'

'Well it will make a change from this place, and we will get to do a lot of shooting exercises and stuff like that.'

I wasn't at all happy. He sounded excited about the prospect of shooting things or people!

'How long are you going to be gone for?'

'Just a week.'

I wasn't sure how to react to the change in his attitude. He hated the army and everything it stood for and yet there he was, excited about shooting. I felt very anxious and insecure, and yet it would be unfair to let him know how I felt, at least, he was happier.

'Well that's not so bad, at least, you will come home the following weekend, not so?'

'Yep, we might even get a few extra days. Hope so.'

He became more like the Boyd I knew once we spoke about our future, my studies, his parents and other non-shooting or army related matters. I was so looking forward to seeing him in a week's time; it felt as though it had been absolute ages since we had last seen each other.

After nearly two hours on the phone with him, we ended the call, with honest and heartfelt declarations of love for each other.

I was still not comfortable with his eagerness about the training camp. It was just so out of character, but there was nothing I could do about it here and now, unfortunately.

Since living in the apartment with Evelyn, I had started going to church on Sundays with her, except when Boyd was home for the weekend. We usually spent the time at his parents' house when he was home.

I had made friends with a lot of the people there, and I felt comfortable among them. I enjoyed the singing the most. Not being able to sing well myself it was wonderful to be able to sing loudly and to know that no one judged me if I went off key a little.

Boyd's new fixation on shooting had unsettled me, and during the church service, I found myself silently praying for him, it was the first time I had seriously prayed about anything. I wasn't even sure if there was a right or wrong way to pray but just talking to God in my head felt right, so I did.

After service one Sunday, I decided to visit my parents since I hadn't spoken to or seen them for some time.

The pathway to the front door was wet but not from any gardening on their part, it had recently rained, and the little plants that rooted in the ground were given a slight hope of producing flowers in the spring. That is if the untamed grass growing into the disheveled flower beds alongside the pathway did not choke them first.

I tapped on the door, opened it, walked in and called out, 'Dad, Mom, hello!'

As I entered the living room from the front hallway there, they were, exactly where I had left them the last time.

How could they go on like this?

Mother was fast asleep on the couch, and my father stared at the TV with a drink in his hand. Both ashtrays were overflowing with stale ash and stompies.

Neither even acknowledged my presence.

I went to my bedroom; I wanted to cry or was I angry?

I couldn't make up my mind. Everything was gone. There hadn't been much in there the last few years when I lived at home, but what was left had been sold, probably for alcohol.

Knowing it would be useless to try and visit with them, I left them a note tied to the bottle of whiskey. I was sure they would get it since it did not look like they touched anything else in the house.

It read: *I came to visit you today, but you were both unaware that I was even here. I won't be coming back again. It hurts me too much when I do. My phone number at the apartment is 934901. If you ever want to see me, please phone me. Kaye.*

As I pulled my car out of the driveway and onto the road, the hurt and pain in my heart overflowed down my cheeks in tears.

Why did my parents do this?

Why did they not love me enough to act like normal parents?

Back in my bedroom at the apartment, I wrote Boyd a letter, not mentioning my parents, though, they weren't worth the mention.

I always felt better writing to him even if it wasn't really about anything in particular. The letter simply held our lives together, symbolic of our connection I supposed.

I also wrote to York since I had received a letter from him during the week. I told him about Boyd's training camp and how he seemed to want to go as it involved shooting a gun. I was concerned about his new attitude. I was very sure Boyd had probably already told York all about it, but it felt good to tell someone else how I felt. York undoubtedly would tell me I was silly and that I should be happy for him. Still, I poured my heart out to him as if he were sitting next to me listening as a good friend would, like the good friend he was.

Chapter Nine

With winter sending its miserable claws biting into my flesh and bones – even though I was in jeans, a thick white polar neck jersey and a padded jacket – at one o'clock in the morning as I waited for the arrival of the bus was not pleasant.

I arrived at the bus stop in Durban as close to the bus' arrival time as possible, not wanting to spend too much time waiting outside in the cold. Until the bus arrived, I sat with the heater on in my car. This year winter seemed to be extensively colder than usual.

The unmistakable lights of the bus made an appearance around the corner of the city hall. I waited until it had come to a standstill in the parking lot in front of the Durban City Hall steps with a loud sounding whoosh and a whine from the hydraulic brakes. The exit door made a swish as it opened and only then did I get out of my car.

The men climbed out of the bus looking half asleep but happy to be home at the same time. Boyd finally put his foot on the asphalt, and I rushed to embrace him as he flung his bag to the ground to complete our embrace.

I was so ecstatic that he would be home for a whole week this time that I had taken a week off from work so that we could relax and enjoy each other for more than just a few hours for a change.

'Missed you so much…' I whispered, and he pulled me into his chest just a little harder, holding me there for just a few seconds longer with his head tucked into my neck. I knew he had missed me too.

We walked back to my car with our arms wrapped around each other, while Boyd mentioned the cold bite that cut the night air and a few other bits of useless information. His duffel bag thrown into the backseat, he settled in the passenger seat; we made our way to his parents' house.

The drive home was rather quiet with a little chatter about unimportant things. I could sense he was very tired and just thought that he would be more talkative once he had a good sleep behind him.

The next day Mrs. Langford made a lunch fit for a king. The huge mahogany dining room table set with all its finery. Pale blue napkins rested on fine dinnerware, on either side of which there lay heavy silver cutlery. The gleaming crystal glassware even made an appearance.

Fresh flowers from the garden were displayed all over the living areas bringing along with them a fresh fragrance. Whenever Boyd came home, the house came alive. Mrs. Langford insisted that the world revolved around her son for the time that he was home.

Although he was still half asleep – I would've gladly let him sleep for longer – he smiled at his mother's efforts, respectfully showing her the appreciation she deserved. But he hardly spoke and was very reserved – more so than usual, presumably because he was so exhausted. He did mention how the time they spent in the bush, even if it was just an exercise, was so physical, and there was very little time to sleep let alone just take a nap.

Boyd told us how the officers were so impressed with his crack shot that they were considering him for greater things.

'But you only have a few months left in your year, what great things do they expect from you?' Mr. Langford asked curiously.

'I am not too sure, but they keep asking if I would join the permanent forces and make a career out of the army.'

I could hardly believe what I was hearing; this was just not the Boyd I knew. The one I knew would never even consider the army as a career. He hated the army. He had told me so a least a hundred times.

'Would you?' I asked, my voice escalating just a little in surprise.

He shrugged his shoulders.

'I don't know, suppose I will just see what happens when it happens…'

Mrs. Langford and I looked at each other, horrified.

'No more talk of the army now. You are here to rest and be yourself,' Mrs. Langford said hoping to cast out the idea of her son shooting people for a living.

It was just too difficult to comprehend Boyd in the army forever.

After lunch we went to Baggies to surf, fortunately being the Indian Ocean, the sea was warm throughout the year.

Boyd looked at the ocean with his board tucked under his arm.

'I miss this; I miss the sea and this beach.'

At that moment, I could see the old Boyd was back, and I felt a bit more relaxed.

It was a humid day in winter. The skies were a hazy blue with sporadic clouds puffing up like cotton balls. The wind was breezy, blowing the clouds so that they changed shape every few minutes.

We were on our boards and in the ocean in no time, joining the rest of the Warner Beach locals, and it felt as if time had not moved on at all and we were still stealing time after school.

With the wind blowing in the right direction, the swell was fairly decent and after an hour or so I was exhausted and very pleased with my attempts to ride a few waves. I made my way back to the beach, a smile on my face. Boyd and most of the other men stayed out until the tide had changed and there were just no more waves left to ride.

I was sitting on my towel at our usual spot in front of the café with a sweater on – it was late in the afternoon, and the sun began to set amid the puffy clouds. My old surfboard rested apartment on the sand next to me as I watched the men fooling around and sharing stories of old days and the waves they had or had not conquered. They were very interested in Boyd's discovery at being such a good shot.

He seemed to find far too much pleasure in giving demonstrations on how he lined up his rifle and took the shot, or how he would hit his target while maneuvering through obstacles. It bothered me.

They ventured from the tables and benches back onto the beach and exhausted themselves with a few games of touch rugby until it was almost impossible to see who had the ball.

A few more of the old local school friends arrived with wood; the fire lit, and we did as we had done so many times before and settled in for an evening around the fire on the beach, the sound of the waves pleasantly crashing in the background.

Boyd snuggled up next to me; he was relaxed and laughing and enjoying this time with all his old friends.

'Pity York isn't here, and then it would be like old times,' he said, staring into the fire as it pulled his gaze into the flames without any effort.

'When last did you hear from him?'

'I got a letter from him last week Thursday. He seems to be enjoying himself. He should be coming home on Friday for a weekend pass. It will be good to see him again.'

'Gosh, I hope he does come home. It will be so good to have my two most favorite men with me again.'

I smiled and nudged him teasingly.

'As long as I am more favored than the other I agree with you,' he teased me back and gently placed a soft kiss on my lips.

It felt so good; I felt so wanted, and it was so perfect that I didn't want him to stop.

He looked at me, guessing my thoughts and kissed me again more passionately and more seriously convincing me of the truth that lay on his lips. His hand came to rest on the side of my face, then moved around my neck securing me in his embrace.

I loved him so much.

When the sun's early morning rays peeked over the horizon, the men with their boards were ready and waited to get into the water and ride waves. The calling of the ocean to anyone that loved to surf was immense and unbreakable. Once you got bitten, you were bitten for good.

York's arrival on the weekend was everything we needed and expected. His sense of humor had outwardly increased while away in the army, so much so that for most of the time spent in each other's company my sides were splitting from laughing so much. I had not realized how much I had missed him and how good it was to see him again.

He still wore his glasses but had filled out around the chest and arms, and it looked as though he had grown at least ten inches.

Needless to say, the weekend spent on the beach with York and a few other men that were home for the weekend on their passes, was an absolute blast.

I dragged Evelyn down with me in the secret hope that she and York would hit it off.

At first, they were interested in finding out more about the other, but the interest soon fizzled out, and Evelyn landed up having fun with Sian much to my surprise. He was never one of the most likable men in the crowd, an extremely sarcastic person with a cynical view of life, and York, well he was York, single as always and funnier than ever.

We were all too afraid to go to sleep in case we became the next victim of one of his hilarious pranks. To match his playful character, he had a contagious laugh that complemented it and once he started laughing it was impossible not to laugh with him.

With York around, Boyd soon forgot all about the army and shooting things, and it was blissful again.

Chapter Ten

Church had become an important part of my life. I found I was drawn to service every Sunday with a passion, to feast on the preacher's words and in particular, the singing. I felt I had a purpose still yet to get discovered. I went with Evelyn to the Wednesday evening Bible study most of the time; the only times I did not go was if an assignment or an exam was on the cards within the next few days.

Boyd rarely went with me to church when he was home on a weekend pass, and I surmised he was either too tired or wanted to spend as much time with me alone, or with his family or surfing.

At last, it was the final day of Boyd's year stint in the army. He had not made his decision about joining the permanent forces or perhaps he had and decided only to tell us once he was home. I prayed endlessly that his decision was not to take the offer.

Mr. and Mrs. Langford waited together patiently and anxiously with me at the airport's arrival gates for Boyd to slip through the doors and into our arms. Mr. Langford had paid for the flight, so Boyd could fly home this last time rather than take the bus.

He walked through the huge automatic doors with his duffel bag slung over his shoulder, and dressed in his step-out uniform He looked every bit the soldier the army intended him to look like, yet on his face, I could see a hint of the carefree surfer boy lurking.

Was that boy back?

Mrs. Langford embraced her son, elated that he was finally home, her elegant green bell bottom pants and cream top melting into him as she held him.

As usual, I waited for him to greet his parents and Holly first, and as usual, it felt like an eternity before I could wrap my arms around him and hold him so close to me that I could feel his heartbeat.

All the way home we spoke about irrelevant things, deliberately avoiding the one question that was on all our minds.

Boyd gave us a detailed account of the party they'd had the night before, and this explained his quiet composure now – very quiet with a splitting headache. Mr. Langford found it extremely amusing.

It was a beautiful summer's day, and Mrs. Langford insisted on having a feast for lunch outside on the shaded patio in the backyard.

Her garden was immaculate, the flower beds around the edge of the garden, in front of the hedges, were all perfectly trimmed and the soil was fluffed up to allow easy breathing for the variety of flowers (practically every color under the sun I was sure) and their roots. The hedges stood upright and rigid as if they stood to attention.

The grass in the center of the garden was so smooth, green and perfectly mowed. I stared at the grass while my over-full stomach relaxed and I wondered how on earth someone got this lawn so smooth and so perfectly even. It was as though someone had rolled the lawn on the ground artificially.

'Rolled on lawn,' I chuckled to myself at the ridiculous idea, 'rolled on lawn indeed!'

I got snapped from my invention theory when Boyd clicked his fingers at me, amused by my far away daze.

'Penny for your thoughts?' he asked giggling at the same time.

I contemplated sharing my invention and then voted against it for fear of sounding stupid.

'Just thinking,' I said, and I knew this would be a good opportunity to bring up the subject of his future.

'So what decision have you made about the army's offer?'

His face immediately became sullen.

'I am not going,' he scowled, 'but they said if I change my mind I must contact them.'

'Why would you want to contact them? You're going to university now!' Mrs. Langford almost sang her response.

I moved from my seat onto his lap in one sliding motion, put my arms around him and hugged him; my fears instantly forgotten.

'Thank you,' I told him.

Mr. Langford stood up and walked to the edge of the patio and let out a heavy sigh of relief and for a few moments just stared at his bare feet.

Those few words from Boyd were like a vacuum released and the oxygen vapourised.

Much later we made our way to Baggies, Boyd was in the surf within a heartbeat of getting out of the car. The waves were not very big, but it was enough for him to relax and to feel at home again.

I was sure it would take a while to get the army out of his system.

He spent his days on the beach or at home while I was at work, and in the evenings, we lazed around my apartment or his parents' house. Sometimes he came with me to Bible study in the week and on most Sundays he came along to church. He did not seem to be very interested in church or the people there, and I felt he did it just to appease me. But I did not deter, one day he might feel like he needed to be there just like I did.

'I don't know what to do with my life,' Boyd miserably uttered as we walked back from the cafeteria at the Amanzimtoti Drive-Inn, our arms filled with foot-long hotdogs, popcorn, chips, and coke. Boyd had plastered a fake smile on his face when he greeted half of the community (the other half were probably at Showboat, dancing the night away).

We got into his car and fixed the speaker securely on the window of his door, making sure the sound was audible, and we began to munch on our food, watching the commercials on the huge screen.

Even though it was already six-thirty in the evening, the February heat was intolerable. My floral summer dress was damp against my sweaty skin, and even my feet were sweating in my sandals, which I then took off. The only thing I could do with my mop of long blonde hair was to tie it up out of my face and off my neck.

He was still not the same Boyd I had fallen in love with so long ago. He was more reserved and more withdrawn than ever. As happy as I was when he'd said he was not going to join the permanent forces, I still wondered how much he meant it.

'Still not decided about what you want to study?' I rested my hand on his and squeezed it lightly.

'Don't pressurize yourself over it. Why don't you leave the studying for next year and rather look for a job this year? I'm sure your parents will understand.'

'I don't know what job I can get. I just don't know...'

He didn't finish his sentence and sighed deeply staring at the movie through the windscreen of the car.

'Do you want to visit your parents tomorrow?' he asked, and I looked at him confused.

'No thanks, I told you I won't go back to them until they phone me. I can't bear to see them in that state anymore.'

'But maybe they won't be like that if you go in the morning?'

Why was he asking about my parents?

He knew the situation with them.

It was so unlike him; I did not know how to understand him. He seemed to be in a stranger mood than ever as the evening dragged along.

I decided to change the subject.

'Have you heard from York?'

'He phoned last night, said the course he was doing is finished now so he should be home by the weekend.'

'That's excellent; it will be good to have him back. I'm sure you have missed him the most.'

I smiled and snuggled into his chest.

'It will be so good to see him. He won't be here for long, though. He said he got offered a further apprenticeship at a big motor company. I can't remember which company he said it was.'

He shrugged his shoulders and sighed again.

The movie was an action movie, one he normally would have enjoyed, but he paid no attention at all. He looked out into nothingness, bleak, miserable and downcast, letting out sigh after sigh, everyone more desperate than the other.

York was still the same old York, happy, funny and he lifted the mood around Boyd so much so that I wanted us to spend every minute in his company.

'I wish you were staying longer. We all miss you, Boyd, most of all.'

I finally had a chance to speak to York on his own. Everyone else was in the ocean surfing, catching the last of the waves the day had offered before the sinking sun brought it to an end.

'Yeah he does seem different, I still can't believe he became this crack shot in the army, it's just so not like him. I would love to stay here and not go back to Pretoria, but I need to get these qualifications. I intend to start my own workshop right here at home one day.'

'Maybe you could offer him a job when you do...' I said, and the sarcasm ran off my tongue like an automatic train.

York chuckled, 'He will get back to his normal self soon enough, you will see, he just needs time.'

He leaned over and nudged my shoulder with his and since I had my arms wrapped around my legs that little shove from York sent my whole body tilting over, and, not being quick enough to get my arms out from my legs in time I fell over like a ball. York burst out laughing while helping me back up. His sense of humor was tireless.

I dreaded saying goodbye to York; I wanted my friend, and I wanted him to stay because he made Boyd feel like the normal Boyd we all knew and loved. I was afraid once he left that Boyd would go back to his melancholy state again, and I did not know how much more of that I could take.

I loved him so much, but while he wallowed in this self-destruction, I was shut out, pushed behind a wall he kept building higher and higher.

Chapter Eleven

With York back in Pretoria and me back at work at the newspaper, I knew Boyd had to get a job soon. If he sat around at home much longer, he would drive himself and everyone else close to him insane.

His father even offered him several positions at his office or via associates, but Boyd turned them all down, finding reasons to decline each one of them.

I asked the manager in the printing department if there was a position for Boyd, even if it was sweeping the floors. He said he would get in touch with me as soon as a vacancy became available.

I prayed morning and evening for this to happen for Boyd, and I even mentioned it to Evelyn and requested her to pray too. She said she would get the ladies on the prayer chain to pray for   him.

It was a week later when Mr. Naidoo phoned me.

'You still wanting da job for your fella? Der one now.'

I practically jumped out of my desk and shouted, 'Oh really! That is so fantastic Mr. Naidoo, thank you, thank you!'

The receiver of the phone was hardly down, and I was phoning his home number.

'Mrs. Langford hello, is Boyd there?'

'Hello, Kaye dear. No, he went surfing as usual.'

She sighed.

'I got him a job here at the newspaper in the printing department, and I wanted to tell him. Will you tell him the minute you see him please?'

'Oh, Kaye dear that is wonderful. I most certainly will. Thank you, dear.'

Mr. and Mrs. Langford were bitterly disappointed that he had not enrolled in university, but I could hear she was delighted he, at least, had a job now.

By the time I got home to the apartment, Boyd had not phoned me back, and Mrs. Langford said she had told him about the job when he got home from surfing. She said he'd gone to his room, had a shower and left.

'Well I'm sure he will be here any minute,' Evelyn said on her way out the door to the Wednesday Bible study.

I went to make dinner; tonight would be steak and chips, Boyd's favorite. I felt certain in my heart things for Boyd would begin to get better. He would become the old Boyd again, and we could start to build our happily ever after from today onwards.

Dinner was ready, but Boyd hadn't arrived.

I wondered over and over what could be keeping him as I paced the apartment from the living room to the kitchen to my room, staring out of the windows looking for him to walk through the entrance of the building.

I phoned his parents' house, at least, three times, and they had not heard from him since he'd left earlier in the day, supposedly to come to me.

The door opened, and my heart sank when it realized it wasn't Boyd but rather Evelyn returning home. She was surprised to hear of my dilemma.

'This is just not like him at all; there must be a very good reason he is late.'

A panic filtered through my veins, I felt jumpy and could not simply sit in the apartment waiting for Boyd – I had to do something.

I went downstairs to my car, got in and drove to the nearest police station in Amanzimtoti. What if he had been in an accident and could not remember who he was?

Maybe he'd had a head injury and lost his memory?

My mind was rapidly filling up with every dreadful scenario.

There were no reports of any accidents with Boyd's description. The very kind constable on duty even phoned all the hospitals in Durban to find out if perhaps he had been admitted.

Nothing!

With the ugly ideas out of my head I drove home, it was nine o'clock in the evening by now.

He will be at home waiting for me. He will be. He has to be!

I walked into the apartment. No Boyd.

Where was he?

'Mrs. Langford phoned to find out if Boyd had arrived, I told her where you had gone, and she said you must phone her as soon as you are here shame, she is so worried.'

I could tell that even Evelyn was now very concerned.

'Her and me both,' I replied, lifting the receiver of the telephone and dialing her number, throwing my car keys into the bowl at the same time.

I phoned Mrs. Langford, who was in bed with a migraine from worrying, so Mr. Langford answered. He too expressed concern over his son's strange behavior, and he too offered various possibilities as to where Boyd might be.

I picked up my keys again, left the apartment and drove around the small towns of Warner Beach, Doonside, and Amanzimtoti. I even drove as far as St Winifreds, stopping at all our familiar places, this I did for at least two hours, fretting, and twice I stopped at a pay phone to phone Evelyn to check if Boyd had pitched up. Everything was in vain, and only confusion reigned.

Worrying about Boyd's whereabouts kept sleep at bay, and even when I did eventually fall asleep, it was a restless, unsettled sleep. The bags under my eyes in the morning were a clear reminder of Boyd's strange behavior the night before.

Today he would show up, and everything would be okay, I could feel it in my bones.

Before I left for work Mrs. Langford phoned, she had still not heard from him and was beside herself with worry. Mr. Langford came on the phone too and was prepared to hire a private investigator if he did not show up by the end of the day. I knew how they both felt.

'Ms. Kaye, did you tell your fella about der job?' Mr. Naidoo asked not even half an hour after I had started work.

'I have not seen him Mr. Naidoo; he had to go away for a few days. Can you hold the job for him, please? I am very sorry about this.'

A little white lie wouldn't hurt.

'No later than Friday Ms. Kaye, no later.'

'Oh thank you very much, Mr. Naidoo, thank you.'

During the day I phoned everyone, I knew Boyd knew. I phoned every hotel and phoned the café at Baggies several times. No Boyd! He was always at Baggies! If he wasn't there then where could he be?

I phoned the police station and all the hospitals again. No Boyd!

When I entered the apartment, I was mentally exhausted. Evelyn kindly made me a cup of coffee and listed her suggestions of possibilities – they all turned up naught.

It was another restless night of endless hours until the sun appeared for another day.

It was the first thought that raced through my head when I woke.

Where was Boyd?

I stumbled into the kitchen for that first cup of coffee, and when I switched on the kitchen light through my sleepy eyes, I focused on a white square on the floor by the entrance door.

I bent to pick it up, and while still on my haunches I lifted it up and turned it over to see to whom it was addressed to. My heart sank, it was so difficult to stand up, and so I just sank onto the floor where I was.

The handwriting on the envelope I could not mistake as much as I wanted to.

It was Boyd's, and I knew this was not going to be something I wanted to read.

With my hands shaking and my heart pounding, I took a deep breath and opened the letter.

I read the short letter, easily deciphering his writing.

Had I read the letter correctly?

I couldn't have, so I read it again. And again. And again. It could not be true! It couldn't be!

'No, No, No! Evelyn…' I shouted.

She came rushing to me also still half asleep wondering what was going on.

I handed her the letter without saying a word. I couldn't speak through the tears cascading down my face while I still sat glued to the floor.

'What?' Evelyn exclaimed, astonished at what she was reading. She read the letter a few times before sitting down on the floor next to me, holding me, cradling me, while I poured out my bleeding heart.

Chapter Twelve

Dear Kaye

I wish I could find the right words to explain what I have to do.

After I got the news of the job at the newspaper I phoned my ex-corporal.
He told me if I immediately left I could go on a mission next week.
I have decided to go.
By the time you read this, I will be on the plane.

I love you so much, but I can't think about doing anything else but going back to the army.

I know this will hurt you, but I do love you, and I hope one day you can forgive me.

Love you
Boyd
xxx

Chapter Thirteen

Amid confusion and hysteria, I managed to brush my teeth, the salty tears blending with the toothpaste. I changed out of my overly large and overly used sleep shirt into a pair of denim shorts and a pink strappy shirt and clambered into my car without shoes or brushing my hair.

I did not care. All I was concerned about was getting to Boyd's parents' house.

Did they know?

The entrance door was flung open, and Mrs. Langford stood aside to allow me in, still dressed in her cotton gown and slippers, a handful of tissues in both her hands all scrunched up and soggy.

They knew!

I burst into choking sobs when I saw the anguished expression creased across Mr. Langford's face.

'This is all your fault, you told Boyd to work instead of going to university, he wouldn't have left if he was at university! It's all YOUR FAULT, YOUR FAULT!' Mrs. Langford yelled at me in an uncontrollable outrage, waving her finger at me like a wild appendage.

'No...I did, no...He went, I never...' I couldn't construct a decent sentence, never mind a rebuttal, but instead spluttered words in shock and horror at the verbal abuse I had just received.

'Verina, don't blame Kaye! This is the army's fault; they did something to our son that totally messed up his head. It is not Kaye's fault!' Mr. Langford scolded his wife with a firm tone of voice, insisting that this was the end of the conversation.

Mrs. Langford ran out of the living room and into her bedroom, slamming the door behind her before throwing herself onto her bed in a screaming fit of hysteria.

'I'm sorry Kaye. I'm sorry for what my son has done to you; you don't deserve to be treated this way after all the time you waited and stood by him. I'd like to give him a blimming good hiding. Please excuse me, but I had better see to my wife before she has a stroke or something. Again, my dear, I am very sorry…'

He stood in front of me for a few seconds convincing me of his sincerity, then he turned and went to console his wife.

I was left stranded in the house, unwanted and alone, unsure and alone, unloved and very much, very much alone.

What was I going to do without Boyd?

He had been everything good in my life for the longest time; I did not know of a future without Boyd.

What was I going to do?

Before I started my car, I sat in the seat, locked the door and blurted out blubbering chunks of crying curses. I had no tissues or anything to wipe my eyes with and used my shirt instead. It got soaked within seconds.

How could Mrs. Langford blame me?

That accusation made Boyd's desertion even worse. I'd just lost my family – the family I hoped I would always have, as long as I lived.

Slowly I made my way home, the car jerking from my shaking legs on the pedals. Everything along the route home bore a reminder of Boyd; we had made the trip so many times together, and we were supposed to make it many more times together.

Why? Why? Why?

Oh, why Boyd, why did you leave?

What happened to you in the army?

I wondered and asked myself a thousand times what could have happened to him to make him change so radically in such a short space of time.

Evelyn, thank goodness, had already left for work by the time I returned to the apartment. She had left me a note with chocolate, voicing in her written words her concern for me. I felt grateful for her and even more so now that I had no one else except her in my life. Everyone important had deserted me in one way or another.

The letter from Boyd was still lying on top of my unmade bed. I picked it up as I flung myself onto the bed and read it again and again, trying to understand what had been going on in his mind and how he expected me just to move forward with my life and forgive him.

Forgive him?

Never!

I would never forgive him for leaving me, for breaking my heart and for leaving me stranded and alone, even causing his mother to turn against me. Now I did not even have any parent – blood or otherwise.

I would never forgive him.

NEVER!

The venom stuck to the voice in my head. I crumpled his letter and threw it to the floor and held the pillow over my chest smothering my heart that was shattering into a million tiny pieces.

I rolled over onto my side, brought my knees to my chest and curled into a ball hugging the pillow for all my sanity, my body shaking as I sobbed and sobbed. The tears poured down my face and soaked into the pillow, drenching it, but I didn't care, I let it all come screaming out of my soul, unable to stop my pain.

When Evelyn came home, I was in an exhausted sleep. She opened my bedroom door gently, and moved softly next to the bed, carefully covering me with my sheets. She picked up the letter from the floor and straightened it out, placing it on the bedside table next to me. She put the ceiling fan on a gentle hum, allowing a breeze to move the heat that hung in the air.

I had a good friend in Evelyn. At least, I had someone to lean on, and I wasn't completely alone.

Chapter Fourteen

I had no choice but to return to work the following day as deadlines waited for no man.

My eyes were as swollen as ripe melons, and when I examined them more closely in the mirror, I could make out the burst veins that spread out over the whites of my eyes. I looked horrific, but I did not bother to put mascara on as they were so swollen, the usually bright green color of my eyes now dull and almost lifeless, filled with despair. Well too bad, I looked how I felt, and by now everyone would have heard about Boyd's cowardly departure, and I just wasn't in the mood for the sympathetic looks and comments that were inevitably going to come my way.

'This too shall pass,' Evelyn said as we headed out for the day, holding onto our skirts as a gust of wind circled the parking lot, teasing our garments willingly.

'You don't owe anyone any explanations, and if you need me, I am just a phone call away.' She gave me a gentle hug before we separated to our cars. Her affection choked me up, but somehow I kept those unwanted tears at bay.

It was a very difficult and trying week, to say the least. By the following day, it seemed as though the whole world knew about my wounded love life.

When I eventually crawled out of bed on Saturday, had a shower and something to eat, the confined walls led me to feel claustrophobic in the apartment. The walls were consuming me, and all I wanted to do was read Boyd's letter over and over again. As my hand hovered over the jewelry box on my dresser where I kept it, it felt as though my hand had a will of its own denying me permission to do what my heart desired. My hand won the battle, and I turned around, grabbed my towel and some change from my wallet, stuffed it into the pocket of my shorts, took my car keys out of the bowl in the kitchen and headed towards my car.

On the beach the sun caressed my tired eyes and pricked my face, revitalizing the skin and its drained pores. I lay on my back on the towel; my knees bent up with my toes digging into the sand over the edge of the towel.

Fully aware that everyone had something to say about me to each other, I didn't care. I just wanted to be here at my favorite place absorbing the wonderful sunshine and allowing the sea to calm my tensed nerves.

It wasn't long when I drifted off to sleep.

The noise of little children playing in the sand at the river mouth that joined the ocean woke me, and I realized it had not been a very long sleep. I sat up and rubbed the sand that had gathered on my legs and took pleasure in watching the children play and the sea directing its own theatrical game.

'Hi Kaye, how are you doing?' Rosalie sat down next to me, her eyes full of questions.

I'd wondered who would be the first to ask.

'Well I'm sure you have heard all about my drama, but I will be okay I guess. I don't know when, but I will be.'

'I know I haven't got the right words to say to you and nothing I say will change anything but do know we're all here if you need us.'

She put her hand on top of mine, squeezing it gently and mincing the sand between my fingers. I didn't know if I should laugh or cry; I felt so useless and pathetic.

'Thank you,' I nodded and chose not to say anything more for fear of losing control.

Rosalie stood up leaving the strong scent of floral perfume wafting around me while her long skirt fluttered in the breeze until she held it down with her hands and walked away back to the rest of the local crowd.

I contemplated going to Mr. and Mrs. Langford's but decided against it as it was too soon after the last time that hadn't ended very well at all. I had not heard from them since that morning and decided I could not bear those accusations from Mrs. Langford again. I would have so dearly loved to have been comforted by her, been held in her arms while she told me her son would get over his silliness and return to his normal self and then all our dreams would become a reality.

If only!

The beach began to bring up too many memories as I watched the surfers in the ocean, so I decided to leave and was greeted by almost everyone as I walked toward my car.

I had to reprimand myself not to be annoyed with them. They were on my side, and just as shocked as I was at Boyd's behavior. No one had seen it coming.

Perhaps next weekend I would hang out with them at the local disco, Showboat. Perhaps? It was quite a possibility that every young adult in the South Coast vicinity went to Showboat on either Friday or Saturday nights or both, some under the required age and some way too old to hang out at a disco. It was a known fact that when the song Je'Taime played, and you were not dancing with a partner, well, then you went home alone and hoped that the next weekend would bring you more luck.

Aimlessly I drove around, feeling hollow and lost, as though I was trying to find my way in a dense fog, and somehow I strangely landed up at my parents' house.

How much I needed them right now!

As I walked up the pathway, there was no change to the landscape, and whatever poor flowers had tried to make an appearance had failed. It seemed symbolic of the family that lived there in a way.

My key still fitted and I opened the front door and walked in. The smell of old cigarettes and dirty ashtrays mixed with spilled alcohol hit me in the face like a cold, wet cloth. It took my breath away. It was disgusting and nauseating, and I could not believe I had come back here and expected things to be different.

Something was different, though; my parents were not in the living room in their usual occupied seats. I walked past the living room and called to them 'Dad, Mom, you home?'

There was no answer, so I went to the kitchen that was on the right side of the house. The sink filled with dirty, grimy dishes and the countertop speckled with empty bottles and glasses. I opened the fridge that was empty except for a bottle of milk and some bits of leftover food.

I walked out of there, holding my hand over my nose and mouth and went past the living room and dining room to the bedrooms on the opposite side of the house. The bed in their room had not been made up; clothes were strewn all over the furniture and floor, the windows and curtains were drawn. I wondered when the last time was that they were opened.

I checked my old bedroom; it was empty, really empty as there was not a single bit of furniture in it. The bathrooms were as disgusting as the rest of the house, but there were no parents at home.

I suddenly had a flash of hope that they were at the shops buying food and cleaning materials. I decided I would phone them later and leave, locking the door behind me but first checking through the garage window and affirming that the car was in fact gone. It was, and I hoped for the right reasons.

Evelyn was out when I got home. I made myself cozy on the couch with the telephone on my lap and phoned York – we had bought ourselves a new long receiver cable that had just come out in the stores, it was wonderful as now we did not have to stand by the phone for the duration of the conversation. It would be really good to hear his voice.

On the promise of seeing each other when he was next in town, we ended our very lengthy conversation. York's surprise at Boyd's career choice and the manner in which he had hurt so many people in the process was as it was for everyone else – shock, anger, and disappointment were a few of the feelings best left unsaid. He felt truly hurt by it too since Boyd, and he had always shared their lives, practically since they were born.

Chapter Fifteen

I felt like a little girl lost in a museum of old vintage trains since Boyd had left. Everywhere I went, or whatever I did there was a cocoon of uncertainty encasing me. I expected him to walk into the apartment or surprise me at work at any minute.

Days became weeks; the months swallowed the weeks, and the longing mixed with pain for Boyd became anger, and that Mr. and Mrs. Langford had shut me out of their lives too made the anger bitter. I was constantly lashing out at anyone or anything. My parents had not responded to my visit, and I decided in my fit of rage to cut them out of my life forever. I was clearly nothing to them so why should they be anything to me?

'Kaye, why don't you come with me to study tonight? You used to enjoy it so much, and you really could do with something positive in your life right now,' Evelyn stood next to me in the kitchen waving a spatula at me as she spoke.

'I don't know; I'm not in the mood for people.'

'Listen to me; this has gone on long enough! Boyd does not deserve the pleasure or honor of destroying who you are. He wins if you carry on being this person and you are not this person.'

Trust Evelyn to be so direct but it was what I needed to hear, and I nodded my head slowly in agreement, or perhaps in fear of the spatula, finally realizing I had to make a new life for myself.

After a delicious meal of spaghetti bolognaise, I went with Evelyn to Bible study.

I sat on my chair hardly speaking or participating in the discussions or hardly listening for that matter, but I did feel better for being there. Everyone was kind, and they were not at all overly concerned with my life as I had imagined they would be. I realized that they had also gotten over the hype of the whole story.

'So you live with Evelyn?'

We had just stood up after the prayer had ended and were picking up our belongings. Some people had already made their way to the urn for tea or coffee. I looked to my right at the man standing next to me.

Had he even been in the class?

I had not even noticed him!

'Yes, and you are?' I raised my eyebrows at him.

'I am Spencer Reed; I've just moved here from East London, this is my second time at this study.'

I probably looked rather confused as I stared at him, wondering why he had chosen me to speak to or why he thought that information would have been important to me.

After a few seconds, I formed a reply, 'Aren't you going to get something to drink?'

Perhaps I was rude I thought and quickly added, 'How did you know I lived with Evelyn?'

'She asked us to pray for you, and I remembered your name in my prayers. Are things better now?'

'Yes,' I said curtly, I did not want to discuss my problems any further with a stranger, no matter how kind he might be.

I turned to get some coffee from the urn, and as soon I took the first step I noticed him following me.

'Can I get you coffee or tea?' I felt obliged to offer.

Before he could answer Darcie tugged his elbow and moved him toward an enthusiastic group of ladies and began introducing him to their gleaming smiles.

I felt relief and disappeared out of the building, to my car and hurried home. Hopefully, by next week, he would be swallowed up by the adoring attention of the ladies and leave me alone. I did not find him that good-looking or appealing, but then again I did not exactly take a good look. The young ladies obviously thought otherwise.

Since my car had to get serviced and was in dire need of some mechanical doctoring, I had to make use of the train to commute to and from work.

It had been a while since I was last on a train, in fact, the last time had naturally been with Boyd when we were still in school. He and York sometimes took the train to go surfing at Addington Beach in Durban.

I sat in the first class section, the green patent leather seats were cold, it was still very early in the morning and even though the sun was up the winter temperatures were frosty. Coming home was a different story as the sun would have baked down on the seats all day and then they would burn your skin as you sat down.

The smell of the railway station, the railway tracks, the sounds of the clickity-clack rhythm, the opening and closing of the doors, the odor of hundreds of people, and the shuffling of their feet intrigued me. I could taste the black grime from the steel wheels and feel the dirt on my skin as I touched the window to open it. I couldn't simply switch off as most people did while they caught up on sleep or read a book. I was fascinated by the sights and sounds.

I was staring out of the window on my way home one evening, looking at the intricate woven tracks along the ground whizzing past that would slowly come more into focus as the train slowed down towards the next station to collect and drop off passengers.

I never paid much attention to whoever sat next to me as I did not want to strike up a conversation; I preferred my solitude and the scenery out of the window.

'Hello,' said the man who sat down, gently putting his backpack between his feet on the floor. His voice sounded familiar.

'Oh hello, sorry I forgot your name.'

'Spencer. How are you?'

'I am fine and you?'

'Good thanks, it's been a long day. You passed me when you got on the train; I saw you were sitting alone, so I decided to join you. I haven't seen you on the train before.'

'No, I'm only using it while my car is in the shop.'

'I can only get a car once the sale of my house comes through next week. It is going to be so great to be mobile again.'

He went on rambling about why he had sold his car rather than drive it to Durban. It is only an eight-hour trip so I could not quite understand his reasoning and I did not want to find out either so I let him carry on with his next bout of rambling, this time about the transfer he had taken to the office in Durban.

'Where do you travel from?' he asked.

'From Amanzimtoti,' I replied curtly.

'I do the whole trip from Durban. Do you know there are seventeen stops from Durban to Warner Beach – Durban, Berea, Dalbridge, Congella, Umbilo, Rossburgh, Clairwood, Montclair, Merebank, Reunion, Pelgrim, Isipingo, Umbogintwini, Pahla, Amanzimtoti, Doonside and Warner Beach.'

He counted them off on his fingers as he listed them.

Why he thought I would be interested in that information, who knew.

I was grateful I only had two stops on my commute. I dreaded the idea of having to listen to him all the way from Durban; seventeen stops from Warner Beach to Durban, with him that would just be too many for my nerves.

We both got off at the Warner Beach station, and he continued to talk all the while. We were hardly up the stairs to cross over the tracks when the clouds opened up to a typical South Coast sub-tropical early evening downpour.

Instinctively we ran across the bridge to our respective lifts, only waving goodbye from a distance.

'Was that Spencer?' Evelyn asked curiously, as I jumped into her car.

'Oh yes, he was on the train. I think he said he is getting a car soon, something about his house, hmm, what did he say again, oh I can't remember. He spoke so much, and I did not listen.'

'He seems a nice person. All the single ladies at church think he is wonderful.'

'I suppose,' I said and kept quiet the rest of the way home.

Every day for the rest of the week Spencer sought me out at the station and made himself my traveling companion. I would rather have been alone staring out the window, and yet he was funny and just did not stop talking, so it was impossible to ignore him.

He was a lot taller than I was and skinny, his hands and feet reminded me of flippers, especially when he expressed himself dramatically with his hands. They flapped about like rubber gloves. His hair was an ash blonde color, and he wore it long, always tucked behind his ears. What probably attracted the women to him was his sky blue eyes. They looked right through you; it was sometimes unnerving. When he spoke his rounded lips exposed less than straight teeth, but they gave him a gentle character. His flair for laughter and his extrovert personality certainly made up for his lack of looks and physique.

He still had to come to terms with the local style of fashion, though. He had to get rid of his tie and chino pants if he ever wanted to fit in with the locals who only ever wore baggies or shorts, jeans, and tee-shirts.

At church on Sunday, he was surrounded by the single ladies, and since I did not have my car back yet, I was reliant on Evelyn for a lift. I would have left immediately otherwise, but instead, I hung around her car waiting for her to finish talking with Sian. They were now dating since meeting on the beach that one time.

'So you've still not got your car back yet?' Spencer asked as he approached me.

'You will be on the train tomorrow?'

'Yes.'

Why did he forever want to talk to me?

For another three days, I had to endure Spencer's non-stop chattering on the commute to and from work.

When I finally had my precious little orange Beetle back, it felt glorious to drive her again, listening to the sound of her engine as opposed to Spencer, was like music to my ears.

And yet I thought of Spencer's chatter all the time. It was as though he had mesmerized my brain to the sound of his voice so that when he was not around, it constantly buzzed in my head. It was annoying.

Chapter Sixteen

My brain and my heart were taking in every word Minister Lyle was saying from his pulpit. It was as if he was summarising the last few weeks of Bible study and as if he was speaking directly to me.

'We can all live forever through Jesus Christ. He died so that we may live; all our sins are forgiven when we accept Jesus into our lives. So I am standing here today a sinner just like everyone else, and I am asking you, what stops you from being saved by Jesus? What stops you from having eternal life? Will your decision here today mean you will live in Heaven forever with our Almighty Saviour, God?'

He closed his Bible, bowed his head and started to pray.

I wiped the tears from my face, and I knew that the niggling feeling I'd had in me since I first started to come along to study with Evelyn was directing me to this moment. I needed to give my life to Jesus.

As the people poured their hearts out in song to God in the final song for the service, I went up to the front row of pews and sat down. I knew there would be plenty of pairs of eyes fixed on me but I was not perturbed, I had a far more important task to do. Minister Lyle approached me and asked how he could assist me.

I told him, 'I need to get baptized.'

My answer was simple, just a few words and yet it was probably the most important few words I had ever said in my life.

After the song, he announced my decision, and I was sure I heard Evelyn rejoicing above everyone else.

The water in the baptism bath at the back of the stage took a while to fill up to the top, which gave me time to rush home and change into a pair of shorts and a tee-shirt and pack a change of clothes for afterward. I felt nervous and excited and all the way to my house and back to the church building I prayed that a fatal accident would not befall me. I needed to give my life to God before I left this earth.

The water was cold and refreshing from the humidity. There were a lot of people hanging around waiting to witness this special moment, most of them were in the Bible study class with me, but there were a lot of the older members too. They loved to see a soul getting added to the Lord's Church.

Minister Lyle stood beside me in the water and asked me a few questions.

I responded, 'Yes,' to all, and then he dunked me under the water so that my entire body got immersed.

I came up a new-born person, washed clean of all my sins and with a new purpose in my life, and a new perspective. I was a servant and a child of God, and I felt elated.

Evelyn stood by with a towel and hugged me as I took it from her, but before she guided me off to get changed Minister Lyle got everyone to hold hands, and he prayed to God for His acceptance of me into His service.

While I changed, I couldn't help thinking of Boyd.

'If only he would give his life to God too, perhaps he wouldn't have struggled so much with himself…' I said to Evelyn sadly.

'You never know, he might just do that one day.'

She put her hands on my shoulders, 'Don't dwell on Boyd; he made his decision, and all you can do now is pray for him and leave it in God's hands. It will be God's Will not yours.'

'Thank you, Evelyn; I would never have found Jesus if it weren't for you.'

I embraced her and held her affectionately, 'You are my sister in Jesus, yay! I have a sister at last.'

We both giggled, and we both knew without saying as much that we were truly sisters, and we loved each other.

I was hugged and kissed on the cheek more times in the half an hour after my baptism than I had been in my entire life. I was beaming and glowing and could not stop smiling.

'Welcome to God's family!' Spencer wrapped his long arms around me and kissed my cheek with a huge smile.

'Thank you; I feel so happy.'

'And so you should, it's the best decision anyone can ever make in their life.'

'When were you baptized?'

'Ten years ago in my swimming pool in Kokstad.'

'Wow, that is impressive.'

'It isn't always easy, the world takes hold of us but as Lyle said, always rely on God and not people to get you through the tough times.'

'You seem to have traveled a lot?'

'Comes with the job. I'm a consulting engineer which means I have to go where my company sends me.'

I looked at him wondering if he had a family somewhere that was waiting for him to get home. He seemed to have read my mind.

'I married once, my wife left me for another man, and that's why I took this position in the company. Travelling helped me get over her.'

My heart swelled with compassion for him.

'Did that happen before or after you got baptized?'

'My wife was never baptized.'

'Oh...' I tried to find the right words to say and then as if on cue I was spoken to by another old lady, and that ended our conversation.

On my way home I made a detour past my parents' house, and on instinct, I pulled into the driveway forgetting the past negative feelings towards them.

As I pulled up into the driveway and got out of my car, my father came out of the house via the back door and down the path between the house and the garage. I was so surprised; it had been such a long time since I had seen him walking and without a drink or cigarette in his hands.

'Daddy?' I said in a surprised tone.

'You need to move your car I must go to the shop,' he grunted.

His words cut through my heart as if edged on a samurai sword. I was so hurt that I was nothing to him anymore and for a few brief seconds, I stared at him, trying to believe that he could be so callous.

'How are you? Is Mom home? I thought I would visit today.'

'Move your car!' he snapped more arrogantly than the first time.

I got into my car and left, the elation of my baptism now deflated, and I had to dig deep into my self-control not to get angry. I remembered what Evelyn had said about Boyd.

'All you can do is pray for him,' and that was all I could do for my parents too.

It still hurt me in bucket-loads though.

I wished I could share my happiness with Mr. and Mrs. Langford but quickly wiped that thought out of my mind or else I would certainly put a damper on my happy day.

I pulled up at a café, and when I was paying for my chocolate, a bunch of flowers was shoved in my face.

'Aaaah!' I squeaked with fright.

Spencer roared with laughter and handed the cash over to the cashier and then handed me the flowers.

'For me?' I asked with even more of a squeak.

'For your special day. I walked in while you were waiting to pay and saw the flowers and well…'

He shrugged his shoulders sheepishly and smiled hoping for my approval.

'Thank you very much,' I blushed.

'I've got a few things to get, and I need to get some petrol before they close at six, so hopefully, I will see you at Bible study.'

He smiled and rushed off to get his things.

I left confused. It had been a day of mixed emotions.

Before going to sleep that night, I thanked God for all that he had given me and for forgiving me. I prayed that the Langfords would also find their way to Him, and I prayed for my parents, and I prayed for Him to use me in His service, but mostly I thanked Him for simply loving me.

Chapter Seventeen

Evelyn had left to spend the university holidays at her parents' house. I hadn't had a reply to any of my letters to Rachel from the day that she'd left for university after school; she clearly was no longer a part of my life, and that left me rather lonely over the Christmas holidays. At least, my friends at church did a lot of social things together so I couldn't exactly become a hermit.

York and I spent a lot of time together while he was at home for a short while. He became very interested in my baptism and even came to Bible study and church with me, and this made me so happy. The days when I wasn't working meant, I spent them at Baggies with York and many of our old buddies.

Boyd's name never got mentioned by anyone, especially not in front of me.

'I wonder if he will ever come back but if he did what state his mind would be in...' York finally said, his curiosity finally out in the open.

'I think I will punch him in the face if I do see him,' I said with a hint of disgust in my voice.

'Hey that's not very Christian of you, you're supposed to forgive remember?'

'Spencer! Hi!' I turned to see Spencer standing next to me looking at the ocean.

'Hey Spencer, howzit,' York said and stretched out his hand to shake Spencer's.

'Sorry, yes, I know I'm supposed to forgive, and I have, but sometimes I just get so angry when I think of what he did to me, and to his parents.'

'Okay so no more talk of Boyd then,' York said as he got up, grabbed his board and made off for the sea and the waves.

'What are you doing on Christmas Day?' Spencer asked sitting down on the sand next to me.

I noticed he had abandoned his outer town clothing and adorned the local attire of shorts and a tee-shirt, it made him look even taller.

'Nothing, York will be with his family, Evelyn has gone to her family, so I'm alone.'

'Well since I'm alone too, how about we celebrate together?'

'Uhm, well okay, thanks. Should we make lunch at my place?'

'Sounds good, my place is always a mess. We can mess up your place together. Cooking I mean, we can mess it up cooking.'

He smiled at his blubbering, and I giggled. I still did not understand why he always wanted to talk to me instead of all the ladies that fell at his feet the minute he walked onto the church grounds.

York came bouncing out of the water a little while later, and I handed him his towel as he reached me. He took it and bent his head just a few inches away from mine and shook it like a dog, spraying water all over me. I covered my face with my hands and laughed out loud. When he was satisfied I was wet enough, he sat on the little bit of my towel I had not occupied and slowly wiggled his way sideways until I had relinquished half of it to him. He looked at me and winked rather smugly, pleased with himself. I was so very content to have York home for a while. I was always in high spirits when he was home.

Spencer tapped on the door and when I opened it he was holding two large bags of groceries and a box wrapped in Christmas paper. It was a wonder he'd managed to knock.

'Merry Christmas,' he said as he handed me the present and, in turn, I handed him a box much smaller than his.

'Merry Christmas to you too,' I replied.

He leaned forward and kissed me softly. I blushed and moved to the kitchen counter and began opening my present. He did the same.

The wrapper was off, and I lifted the lid of the box carefully.

'Oh, it's gorgeous. I love it!'

I held the cuddly white teddy bear with the reddest nose and hugged it to my chest, loving it immediately.

'Shoo, so glad you like it, I had no idea what to get you. So now what's in this box?'

He lifted the lid, and I held my breath hoping he would like the box set tapes of the Moody Blues.

'Oh wow this is fantastic, oh man thank you, Kaye, really thank you!'

He leaned toward me and gave me another kiss. I blushed and fussed over my teddy bear rather than look him in the eye.

'Shall we cook?' I asked, deliberately breaking the moment.

We made an average tasting lunch of fried chicken, rice and veggies. Conversation flowed easily between us, and he told me more of his failed marriage – there were no children for which he was grateful – and I told him my side of the Boyd affair. It was as if we were old friends catching up after not seeing each other for a long time.

For dessert, we had ice-cream and chocolate sauce which we were busy eating when York arrived. Lunch with his family was a quick affair.

'Hey Spencer, howzit, Merry Christmas,' he said and shook his hand.

'Merry Christmas Kaye,' he leaned forward and kissed me.

I didn't mind him kissing me; I was used to the peck of a kiss we gave each other. He handed me a little box.

'Merry Christmas, York.'

I handed him a large soft present. We opened them together - I opened, he ripped.

I gasped, 'York it's too beautiful.'

I lifted up a delicate silver cross that hung on the finest silver chain. I handed it to him and turned around lifting my hair so he could put it on for me. I patted it with delight as it fell on my chest.

'It's so beautiful, thank you.'

I smiled at him and then had the pleasure of watching him pull out the variety of things in his package – shirts with funny cartoons printed on them, Bob Marley tapes, and a leather neckband with a shark's tooth attached to it. The last one he'd had got lost in the sea.

'Kaye this is awesome I love it all, thanks, chicky.'

He turned around and lifted his blonde locks off his shoulders in a mocking fashion so that I could put the necklace on him. He gave me a kiss and a wonderful hug.

'You want some ice-cream?' I asked as York joined Spencer in the living room.

'What you think?'

He smiled at me, and all I could do was laugh and get him a large full bowl.

York and Spencer got on well; they found common ground in cars and surfing. Spencer had started surfing while living in East London and like it had done to others, it bites and sticks with you.

Chapter Eighteen

York left two days after New Year's day. We had the usual beach party to see the New Year in and spent as much time with each other as was possible. Spencer became one of the crowd as he slowly progressed with his surfing skills. He even came to visit me on a more regular basis.

When York walked through the boarding gate at the airport, my heart was heavy, aching for the close friendship we shared, but Spencer was waiting at the entrance to the apartments with a bunch of flowers when I arrived home from the airport.

'I knew you would be feeling sad so I thought the flowers would cheer you up,' he smiled as if pleased with himself for being so thoughtful.

'That is so sweet, thank you, they are lovely.'

I invited him in for coffee; his company would be just the thing I needed right now.

It was a beautiful, autumn Saturday, and rather than stay indoors Spencer mentioned that some of his work colleagues were playing in a soccer match at Hutchison Park in Amanzimtoti and suggested we go and watch. I quickly changed into a pair of Gap denim bell bottoms and a red checked shirt and put on my very high corked wedged shoes. Perhaps not the best shoes to wear to a soccer match but I was at least almost as tall as Spencer with them on.

I was sure the entire communities of the South Coast were all there. The game was exciting and naturally well supported by the local crowd. We sat on the bank alongside the field among our familiar friends and joined in with the occasional yell at a referee or a player and, of course, we all cheered wholeheartedly when our team scored a goal.

There were several games played throughout the day, and so we ended up being there the entire day, eating hotdogs, drinking cool fizzy drinks and thoroughly enjoying the company of each other as well as our friends.

On the way back to his car, Spencer took my hand and linked his fingers with mine; I didn't withdraw my hand. I knew where we were going with this, and I was ready, if not a bit hesitant, to take that leap.

Although I was still confused and hurt by him, I had by the Grace of God forgiven Boyd and allowed my heart to open up to a new relationship. Perhaps Spencer was the one God wanted me to be with; I had to allow myself to get led by God and not my emotions. I silently prayed this was what God wanted.

When we reached the car parked under the huge evergreen trees, Spencer still held my hand. He looked about him contemplating if this was the right moment to say what it was he wanted to say.

'Kaye, can we go out together, I mean like always?'

He blushed nervously.

'I'd like that, yes,' I giggled as I replied, blushing too.

He put his arms around me, his face bent toward mine, his magnetic blue eyes pulled me toward him, and he kissed me gently.

It was not a kiss that made me shiver with delight as Boyd's had always done, but it was pleasant. Perhaps it was just me and the reservations I still harbored toward any man since Boyd.

He kissed me on the forehead and pulled me into him in an embrace. I felt content in his arms. I supposed the kissing would get better as the relationship progressed.

I was growing with the Lord every day. Spencer and I never missed a study or service on Sundays. The single ladies were a little disappointed Spencer was now "taken" but we were all friends and so jealously was not an option.

We had become inseparable while we developed our relationship with each other as well as with God.

The kiss still did not have the fireworks that girls dream of, but he made up for that in the way he cared and with his bubbly personality.

The phone rang while we were watching the Saturday movie on TV. Evelyn got up and answered it as she was closest.

'Hello,' she said, then listened for the reply from the caller for what seemed like a second and then she handed the phone to me, pulling the long cord almost to its capacity.

'It's for you.'

'Hello?' I said.

'Is this Miss Kaye Raines?' the voice asked.

'Yes. Who is speaking?'

'This is Constable Kruger from the Amanzimtoti Police.'

I straightened and motioned to Evelyn, who was still standing to turn the TV down.

'Your parents live at 34 High Road, yes?'

'Yes,' I replied hesitantly, not liking the direction this was taking.

'Please, would you come to their house immediately? I'm afraid there has been a fire.'

'What? Are they okay? How bad?' I asked, and without taking a breath or waiting for an answer, I put the receiver down and stood up, heading for the bowl of keys.

'Come with me please, there was a fire at my parents' house I think,' I said rushing toward the door, Spencer and Evelyn already following me.

Spencer's car was the easiest to get to, and he drove as though the devil was chasing him. In minutes, we drove into High Road to a scene from a movie.

It was dark already, and the streets soaked in water, and yet it wasn't raining. The reflection of the street lamps and the flashing red and blue lights gleamed off the water, and the footsteps of the people and firefighters everywhere splashed in the water as they rushed to and fro.

I could hardly breathe as I saw the number of big red fire trucks, many smaller ones too and a collection of emergency vehicles parked outside the house of my parents. There were so many people bordering the barrier tape that was sectioning off the problematic area that we had to fight our way through the curious bystanders.

Ducking under the barrier tape, a fireman, clad in his yellow safety attire that looked heavier than he was, came up to me quickly intending to prohibit me from entering the danger zone.

'Sorry, ma'am you cannot come through here.'

'It's my parents' house…' I choked out, and before he could stop me, I grabbed Spencer and Evelyn's hands and ran toward the house, jumping over several hosepipes that lay on the ground then stopping in my tracks the instant I had a clear view of the house.

I turned around and looked for someone that looked as if they were in charge; I couldn't make out anyone in particular, there were just so many people dressed in firemen's thick and heavy yellow suits. Medical men in their red overalls and also several policemen in their blue uniforms, and so I kept running toward the house. I was only wearing a pair of flip-flops, so my feet and my legs were drenched with water, but I didn't care, I only cared about getting into the house.

'Ma'am! Ma'am, please you can't go in there, please ma'am!'

A paramedic had me by the arm preventing me from running any further. Spencer and Evelyn obviously believed him as they held me back too.

I began to shout and fight them all to break free to continue with my quest to get into the house. To find my parents, to make sure they were okay, to make sure they were still alive.

'NOOOO LET ME GO! MOMMY, DADDY – LET ME GO. LET ME GO.'

A man with a shiny badge on his wet uniform and two police officers approached me while the others still held me back with difficulty.

'Miss Raines, please come with me so I can explain all of this to you calmly.'

The man with the badge led me to the back of an ambulance and sat me down, Spencer and Evelyn in tow along with the policemen.

The paramedic gave me an injection that frightened me as the needle penetrated my skin. I was not even aware he had taken my arm to administer it.

'Ouch!' I yelled and tried to get my arm back.

'Miss, it is to keep you calm, trust me on this.'

He looked at me pointedly; I felt so confused.

'Miss Raines, it seems one of your parents fell asleep with a cigarette still lit, and it set the house on fire. I am sorry, but your parents did not survive the fire.'

'WHAT? NO NO NO!'

I attempted to get up, run and drag them out of the house; they had to be still alive. They had to be.

'LET ME GO. LET ME GO....Please please let me go!' I begged, choking out the words.

The medication injected into my arm had started its process, and I was feeling slightly woozy. Spencer held me with his arm wrapped around me so tightly I had no escape.

'I am so sorry Miss Raines, please know they would not have suffered at all. They were sleeping and would not have known their fate.'

The kind man held my hand, stroking it with his other hand and I felt his sorrow. For an instant, I tried to imagine what he must've seen when he'd entered the house and found my parents. I shuddered and dismissed the visuals immediately.

'If you need any more information please don't hesitate to contact me. Again I am very sorry Miss Raines.'

He handed a card to Evelyn and left. I looked up at the house, and with the lights from the rescue trucks and street lights all, I could make out was a portion of the house on the right. It seemed everything else had collapsed.

Evelyn confirmed with the paramedic that I was able to leave, and Spencer lifted me gently, putting his arm around me, steadying my wobbly legs. He helped me to the car where he slowly moved me onto the back seat and sat next to me, my head leaning back against the headrest as I stared out at the burnt house, weeping. Evelyn climbed in behind the steering wheel fighting the tears that wanted to fall out of her eyes as she drove us home.

Chapter Nineteen

Why did I not teach them the gospel?

Why did I not visit them more often?

Can God forgive me for being angry at them?

Why would they not love me enough to change?

Why this and why that I asked myself over and over again relentlessly.

The news was by now all around town as well as all the neighboring towns. The phone in the apartment would not stop ringing, Evelyn had barely put the receiver down when it would ring again. Eventually, we let the receiver rest on the table so we could have some peace.

I was numb.

Could this have happened to my parents?

Spencer and Evelyn both took a few days off from work to be with me, and I was so grateful to lean on them, especially when the phone calls to the relatives had to be made.

Minister Lyle was kind and supportive, offering to take over the arrangements for the memorial service for me and to deal with the undertakers.

'Don't blame yourself for the demise of your parents, Kaye. You were their responsibility, not the other way around. They made the choice to live the way they did. God sees your heart, and he knows how you tried to visit with them and to have a relationship with them.'

'But I drove away, and in anger, I cut them off from my life. If I had maybe insisted on talking to my dad that day instead of just driving off, maybe it would have been different.'

'Kaye, you can't dwell on what-ifs. Everyone has a choice. They chose that lifestyle; they knew God's Word. Remember they were Christians before they inherited their wealth. There was no need for them to walk away from God but they chose to. There was not much you could have done for them. They had to do the changing, not you. All you can do Kaye is pray that God has mercy on their souls.'

When Minister Lyle left, and after a rather heated debate, which I finally won, Spencer, Evelyn and I took a drive to the house. I wanted to see the house as soon as possible if I waited it would keep me awake at night until I did.

It was a horrible sight. The ash floated about as the breeze blew and that smoke smell attacked us as we came near the house. I felt sorry for the neighborhood.

The barrier tape was still up, and a few officials were lurking about the property. I ducked under the tape, my body a mess of jitters and wobbly legs, and Spencer and Evelyn followed closely behind. As soon as we reached the remains of the house, a gentleman enquired as to who I was and what was I doing there. Once I explained it all to him he begrudgingly let me stay, but he was never too far away from me, keeping an eye on everything that I touched.

There was one wall left standing, the wall with the back door on the right side of the house. The frame of the door seemed to be suspended on invisible hinges as it stood very rickety in the half-burnt wall. Everything else was burnt down to the ground. I could not determine what was furniture or what was the actual building.

As I walked through the rubble and carnage that once was a house, crunching under my feet, I had a feeling I might just walk over my parents' burnt bodies. It gave me the complete shivers and shakes that I ran from the burnt remains as fast as possible, tripping several times over charred pieces of wood and pieces of metal jutting out in my path.

I rubbed my legs as I ran from the rubble trying to get the ash off that had stuck onto me.

'Get off, get off, get off….' I repeatedly pleaded rubbing my legs as I ran, which hindered the movement causing me to stagger and lose my balance. Spencer caught up with me and with the edge of his navy blue shirt, he rubbed off any ash that got left on my legs, assuring me, calmly and soothingly, that it was all removed before I attempted to walk the rest of the way back to the car holding onto him, trembling. I had to admit to myself that it was, in fact, a very stupid thing to have come here, to this place of ruin and devastation.

On the way back to the car I noticed a marigold in the flower beds alongside the pathway that was struggling to survive among the ash and grime from the fire. I picked it out of the ground, thinking that it might have a chance to survive once I replanted it in a pot. This little flower was the only physical reminder I now had of my childhood home.

York flew in for the day Minister Lyle with a handful of relatives held a small ceremony. It was not emotional or dramatic, what can a person say about people that had turned their backs on God and their family? The relatives whom I could hardly remember stayed after the service for refreshments and a few snacks and then left. That was the last I saw or heard from them.

'Wish I had been here for you these past days and that I didn't have only one day, I'm a bad friend; I'm so sorry…' York pleaded.

'Don't talk like that York, I understand it's difficult for you and there wasn't anything you could have done, there wasn't anything anyone could have done. But you are here now, and that's all that counts.'

When he put his arm around me, I felt so at ease, and all my sorrows, worries and emotional baggage were swept away by his arms. In York's arms, I was safe from all harm. To feel this safe again, I would have to wait until December.

Once I had completed a few weeks of counseling with Minister Lyle, I managed to get to grips with the guilt I felt over my parents. I had to concentrate on my life and my walk with the Lord. Not forgiving myself would hinder my faith and my salvation. 'God died for your sins, and forgave us all for our sins. How small do I make Him when I can't forgive my parents or myself?' I would ask myself aloud.

It was comforting to have Spencer as my boyfriend, he was by my side, supporting me throughout this difficult time. I felt I was in love with him. He deserved for me to love him.

But it was in my dreams when I had no control over my mind that everything fell apart and that I suffered the most.

The first week after the fire I would wake up in a cold sweat from the crazy nightmares. Most times I would wake up screaming which brought about uncontrolled sobbing and would most of the times wake Evelyn. She would rush to console me and calm my shaking body. I felt so bad as she needed the rest as much as anyone did.

In my dreams I was running away from my zombie parents, the faster I ran, the faster they came upon me, groaning and making the freakiest sounds, their arms outstretched just a fingertip away from grabbing me. No matter how long or how far I ran I never got further than the burnt offerings of the house. Just before they would catch me, I always woke up. When I eventually fell asleep, again the same vivid images of my burnt parents wreaked havoc with my subconscious. It was exhausting.

I buried myself in my work, in my studies and Bible study, and slowly the nightmares became fewer. It was many weeks before I realized I had slept through the entire night without waking up once, without any dreams of dead parents chasing me in my head.

Minister Lyle was delighted to hear this.

'Pray, pray, pray. Never cease praying, Kaye. With God, you can conquer anything. Even zombies!'

He laughed and more than anything I appreciated his candor and burst out laughing with him.

Chapter Twenty

Spencer and I were having pancakes at Peter's Pancakes in Amanzimtoti on an autumn evening.

'I know we haven't been dating for years, but I don't want to waste any more time.'

He pulled out a little black box, blushing like a crimson rose, with a smile that covered his face and with his hands shaking he presented the box to me.

'Marry me, please?'

Everyone in the restaurant stopped eating, the clinking of cutlery and crockery went silent, and everyone paid attention to our table, to Spencer, and waited in anticipation for my reply. The entire restaurant held their breath.

Taken by such surprise; my green eyes turned to emerald as the color of my face matched that of Spencer's. I took the little black box and held it in my hands, looking at his expectant face nervously waiting for my response.

My heart fluttered excitedly, it was right that I should accept him, he was a good, kind man and he loved me. He told me every day he loved me, and when I needed him most, he stood by me, and above all he loved God.

I would never be unevenly yoked, so why was I hesitating; because I was stupid, that's why!

'Would you rather be alone for the rest of your life?' I reprimanded myself.

'Yes!' I said, and every patron in the restaurant exclaimed happily and clapped their hands while Spencer stood up and leaned over the table and kissed me.

'Thank you,' he whispered with his kiss.

I took the little gold ring with its shiny diamond out of the box and gave it to him to put on my ring finger. It fitted perfectly.

'So when do you want to get married?' I asked.

'It's all up to you love, whenever and however you want. I will go along with anything as long as you are happy.'

'Can we have a December wedding, then York can be here? I will phone him tonight, and it's also before Evelyn goes on university holidays too.'

'I'll ask York to be my best man; I'm sure Evelyn will be your bridesmaid.'

'Please, can we keep this a very small affair? No more than the very closest people in our lives.'

'That suits me fine, the only people I will invite anyhow will be my boss and my folks, but with my dad being so ill they probably won't be able to make it.'

He kissed me once more as he leaned over the table again.

When we walked into the apartment, Evelyn and Sian were playing scrabble at the small four-seater dining room table, and I put my hand over hers.

'Notice anything different?' I said giggling, the single diamond gleaming as brightly as my smile.

'Oh my goodness, you finally did it, Spence! I'm so happy for you Kaye, so happy!'

Evelyn stood up and threw her arms around me, our bodies swaying together as she hugged me.

'This is so exciting,' she said as she pulled away from me eventually, and lifted my hand to hers to have another look at the ring.

'You knew about all this?' I asked surprised.

'Of course, Spencer had to ask advice as to whether I thought you would say yes or no and what type of ring you would like et cetera.'

They exchanged glances and smiled at each other clearly proud of themselves.

'Will you be my bridesmaid?'

'Will I?' She squealed throwing her arms around me again and, this time, swaying me so excitedly I nearly lost my footing that almost sent us both falling over onto the floor. Somehow we managed to find our balance with much jubilance and laughter.

Evelyn took notes until almost midnight of all my ideas, thoughts and opinions regarding the wedding. We even had the guest list sorted already. The only thing keeping her from planning the entire wedding down to the color of the napkins was York. In the morning I would phone him, it was too late now, to find out when it would suit him.

I felt a little anxious about telling him for some reason.

'You're doing what?' he asked as if he hadn't heard me correctly.

'You sound shocked? It is the natural next step. He wants you to be his best man.'

'He does? Sorry, I am an idiot. Congratulations chicky, I'm happy for you. You of all the people I know deserve to be happy. So when is the wedding?'

'When are you coming home in December? I'm planning it around your plans, so you better be here.'

'Well I am the best man you know,' he chuckled smugly, 'I should be home about the ninth.'

'Good, then the wedding will be on the fifteenth. Is that okay with you?'

'It's not up to me chicky, it's your day, so any day is good for me.'

I could hear him smiling on the other end of the phone.

'Good, then it's the fifteenth.'

'How are you doing chicky?'

'I'm okay, some days I get angry and confused. My parents' death seems to have stirred a lot of the Boyd anger in me. I thought I had it under control but clearly not.'

'If I ever see him again I will knock his block off; I promise you.'

'He will probably shoot you!' I burst out laughing at my wit.

York found it funny too, and we had a good giggle over the phone.

'So here is something you will like to hear…'

Then he keeps quiet, toying with my curiosity.

"What? Come now, tell me.'

'I found a church here like the one you go to; I've joined their study class as well.'

'Oh my goodness, that's wonderful news! I am so super happy right now.'

We chatted a bit longer before I realized I had run up the newspaper's telephone bill by about thirty minutes. Hearing that York was committing his life to God just made me so happy. No, happy was too mild an expression, thrilled was more like it. I wanted to sing in my false apartment voice and rejoice as loudly as I possibly could, but not in the office; they would never understand.

Once Evelyn knew the date she went into fast mode. I had to do nothing but approve colors and designs.

The sale of the property that my parents' house had stood on took longer than usual to sell. The stigma attached to it put most people off buying it. Eventually, a foreigner bought it for far less than what it was worth. But once it was sold, I could file another bad and unhappy memory away for good.

The five thousand Rand that came to me, after all, the expenses got paid went toward the wedding, the honeymoon and my studies. I could now finally finish my degree in journalism. Spencer, my boss Rodger, Evelyn and York tried to convince me to buy a new car as well, but I just could not think of parting with my baby Beetle. She had been my first car and had hardly given me any trouble. She was reliable and in my opinion, far more reliable than a lot of people I knew and she held onto the dreams I buried deep within me. She was worth more than gold to me, and I was keeping her!

Chapter Twenty-One

Planning the wedding did not take much effort since only thirty people were attending. Spencer's parents were indeed going to make the trip in spite of his father's health. Then there were our friends from the Bible study, my boss Rodger and his wife, Spencer's boss and his wife and that was it.

The auditorium at the church building was more than large enough, and with a little blue decor, in no time, it looked like a reception hall.

It was a humid, muggy and overcast Saturday. The rain not forecast, but the clouds were dark and ominous.

'Come on Kaye, Sian is here to take us to the church!'

Evelyn was fussing about her dress, picking up the flowers and instructing Sian to take the bags we each had with our change of clothes in, to the car.

'Almost done!' I yelled back.

I put my white strap stilettos on and took a last look at myself in the mirror, checking that the twirls in my hair had not come out and that my plain basic makeup had not smudged. The image before me I had seen only once before – so fancily dressed up – and that had been some years ago at my Matric Dance.

'A lifetime ago...' I muttered to myself before my heart hurried down that path of regret.

I straightened the A-lined skirt of my white chiffon dress with its V-neck lace bodice and checked that the long, wide laced elvish style sleeves had not caught onto anything and left loose threads. The long lace train Evelyn would connect to the dress at the church.

Where was the train?

I looked around the room and failed to see it anywhere. My heart starting to beat faster, I looked all around the room again, lifting the pillows, the bed quilt cover, the towels that were lying over the chair. I even checked the cupboards. I still couldn't find it.

"Evelyn, have you seen my train?' I yelled, still looking around the room.

'You asked me to keep it with the flowers so you wouldn't forget it. I have it. Are you ready? We must go!'

I sat on the bed, waiting for my racing heart to stop running away and creasing my dress all over again; I tried to reassure myself, 'Just calm down silly woman. It is natural to be so nervous. You're going to have a beautiful wedding, and you're going to live happily ever after. You have a wonderful fiancé who loves you and who loves God. With Spencer, you can have God at the center of your marriage. Just calm down!'

I let out a long deep breath; it was now or never.

'Kaye come on,' Evelyn came bursting in the bedroom, 'what's wrong?'

'Nothing, I just panicked when I couldn't find the train. I'm ready, let's go.'

'You look beautiful Kaye, absolutely stunning.'

She smiled and reached out her hands towards my tiara to adjust it ever so slightly so that it sat perfectly centered on my up-styled hairdo; then she fluffed up my veil. She ran her hands down my arms till she found my trembling hands

'You are just stunning my friend, now let's go.'

I looked at this tall redhead with skin that was almost permanently pink but not unattractive by any means and was so grateful she was my friend, my sister in Christ.

The silver and pearl necklace I had given her in gratitude for being my bridesmaid hung on her chest shining brightly against the royal blue chiffon dress. Her eyes were blacker than usual. I was always fascinated by her unusual combination of black eyes and red hair.

'Come on ladies, your chariot awaits, tick-tock, tick-tock!' Sian yelled from the doorway.

We lifted up the skirts of our dresses and made our way to the car that would be our carriage to get us to the church not on time but at a respectable time - on my time.

Spencer stood tall, taller than usual, at the front of the church, in a dark blue suit. He looked very dashing and nervous. York stood just as smartly dressed beside him, and I noticed his adoring smile as my eyes flicked between the two men's faces.

The walk up the aisle seemed longer than when we'd rehearsed it, or perhaps it was the long train that slowed my walking.

With everyone's eyes focused on me I wished I had someone that was alongside me whose hand I could hold. My knees were shaking with every step I took in the high heels, and I thought I might fall over at every next step.

Each pew was graced with a bouquet of white roses, blue irises, and orchids, flooding the church with their fragrance.

When I finally reached Spencer I was hot and could feel the perspiration pricking my forehead; a nervous smile plastered on my face. He took my hands in his, and we walked to the edge of the stage steps together, unable to stop staring at each other. I wondered if my makeup was running down my face and hurriedly turned to Evelyn and whispered for her to take a quick look. She smiled and winked at me indicating that I was as I should be. A blushing bride.

Minister Lyle gave a short service that was light-hearted and rather witty which suited me and lifted my nerves off their tendrils.

Spencer looked at me with his piercing blue eyes, right into my heart.

'I do,' he said when prompted by Minister Lyle.

I said 'I do' when it was my turn, and then we kissed, sealing our commitment and hearts to each other forever.

After a few photos had been taken in the colorful gardens of the church grounds and under the black skies, I took the long train off the dress before we went to the reception. It was just too long and was more of an irritation than anything else.

'You are so beautiful my wife, I love you,' Spencer held me for the brief moment that we had to ourselves on the way to the reception.

'I love you, my husband,' I smiled lovingly back at him and relished the kiss he passionately gave me, cupping my face in his hands.

The intimate moment was interrupted by Evelyn calling for us to join the reception.

Speeches were short and brief. York made me spill a few tears as he asked everyone to raise their glasses to toast the bride. He gave a little speech about how long we had known each other and the difficult times I had been through – without mentioning any of it – and how much he cared for me and would always be my first friend.

All the first dances were over with, and Spencer and I had danced well together, our feet moved timorously without tramping on the other's toes. The two-tiered cake decorated with blue irises was cut, and it was finally time to relax, to change into normal clothes and to be Mrs. Reed.

I danced all night with either Spencer or York. I laughed so much with everyone. I was exhilaratingly happy.

We finally left the reception through a human tunnel to Spencer's car for a honeymoon of five days in Margate on the South Coast.

While we were making the one-hour journey, Spencer said, 'So I have a little surprise for you Mrs. Reed, hmmm I do like the sound of that, Mrs. Reed.'

He chuckled.

'Really, what is it?'

'On Thursday my boss called me into the office.'

He looked at me briefly with a huge smile before focusing back on the road. It was dark, already ten o'clock but at least, there was very little traffic, if any, the entire journey.

'Yes, and?'

'I have been promoted. My boss thought it would be a nice wedding present. I am now a senior consulting engineer. It comes with more benefits and a sizeable increase too.'

'That's so wonderful Spencer; no one deserves it more than you do, well done!'

I reached over and kissed him on the cheek.

'Why are you only telling me now?'

'Well, it's been so hectic with people forever being around us, and last night I wasn't allowed to see you, so I thought it best to wait until we were on our own. You happy, my love?'

'I am very happy Mr. Reed. Very happy indeed.'

After five days of a blissful honeymoon, we were back in the land of the living at Spencer's apartment that was not too far from Evelyn. She and Sian had moved my few belongings to my new home while I was away.

Our first weekend together as husband and wife was spent buying necessary and unnecessary items for our home. Our tastes were vastly different, but somehow we found common ground by sticking to neutral colors for the furniture, curtains, and linen. There was not a lot of decor in our apartment other than a single large framed photo of our wedding day that we hung on the one bare wall in the living room.

Chapter Twenty-Two

Spencer was kind and loving. We prayed together every morning and evening and made our plans for the future with God. We had a five-year plan all nicely decided. We'd welcome children in the fifth year, and until then we would stick to our plan and build our nest egg.

York had moved without leaving a forwarding address or a contact number. It worried me, and it hurt me so much that he would just leave as Boyd had done. I phoned everyone and every place I knew of to try and track him down, but no one offered any information. It felt as though they had been instructed to keep his whereabouts in the dark.

Why?

Once again in my life, I was so confused, I had always been so convinced we would be friends forever. Everything he said at my wedding had been so touching and affectionate – had that been a lie too? Was he no different to Boyd? He had broken my heart now too, just as Boyd had done. As if I never had enough unanswered questions to ponder on, now he had to add to the load.

All I had left now were Spencer and Evelyn. Perhaps this was the way the Lord wanted it to be, and so I convinced myself of its truth. I had no reason to think otherwise.

Everything else in our lives went on as usual. Evelyn and I met up with each other as much as possible, and Saturday mornings became a regular visiting time for a few hours, shopping, having coffee at the Wimpy in Amanzimtoti or simply visiting at each other's homes but we always kept our date.

Spencer's working hours increased as the months flew passed. He was having to leave earlier in the mornings and worked on most Saturdays, hence, the time I had to spend with Evelyn. Slowly it progressed to some evenings, and then he would also bring his work home. I didn't mind as it was his job and he was a perfectionist, but it just got very lonely sometimes, and even when he was at home and not working, he was very quiet and lost in his thoughts. I presumed it was his work that occupied his thoughts so much, preventing him from speaking nonstop over irrelevant matters, like the old Spencer I'd grown to love.

At Bible study and church he was his normal friendly self, and once we got home, he remained that person, but only for a while. He would revert to the silent Spencer once he had been back at work the following day.

I was finally being sent out into the field to cover a few editorial stories at work. Having received my degree earlier in the year, I was now ready to embrace the world of journalism. My boss Rodger was keen to get me going on a few local stories, nothing too dramatic or intense, and I was gradually led into those. I made a few friends at the police station and in the emergency rescue teams, including the firefighters. They all remembered me from my parents' fiasco, and that helped tremendously.

Very soon I was the first on their list to call when an emergency occurred. It spiked my adrenaline to a point where I thrived on it, and it became like a drug, so much so that sitting in the office doing admin work was like living in a nightmare. This new direction my vocation had taken kept the hours at home without Spencer, or even with the silent Spencer, more manageable as I dove into my work. The spare bedroom became our study in which we both spent more time there than any other room in the apartment. At least, we were in there together doing what we both loved.

'Do you think you are ready for a big scoop?' Rodger asked one day, leaning against the edge of the partition of my cubicle, being very careful not to lean too hard so that it fell over.

'Oh for sure! What's the story?' I was suddenly wide awake and all ears.

'There is going to be some trouble at St Alban Prison in Port Elizabeth. A little birdie told me that something big is going to happen over the weekend when all the big shots are there for the annual budget meeting. Will you be able to go for the weekend and longer if you need to?' He was clearly chuffed at this inside information he had received, and I was elated that he had chosen me. I did not mind where or what the situation was or what day of the week I was needed.

'Of course, I can go, that's my job isn't it?' I replied with a smile strapped around my ears, immediately packing up my desk.

'That's my girl. Kiki will be your photographer, and I will get my secretary to arrange the flights and hotel bookings immediately. You leave tonight.'

'Thank you for everything Rodger; I won't let you down.'

'You better not, now get going before I give the story to someone else,' he grinned and walked away.

While I waited for my flight and hotel bookings to be confirmed, I phoned Spencer. Luckily he was in his office, although he was almost out the door and had to back up to take the call.

'You're not going to be in any danger are you?'

'No, I doubt it.'

'Well, it is good for your career, well done. I won't see you until next week then.'

'Depends on how long the incident carries on for, I might be home on Sunday even.'

'Probably, but I'm going to miss you. I have to go. Love you.'

'Love you too.'

Setting the receiver in its place I realized we had become a career orientated married couple, it suited me, though, since he did not want children soon and what else was I supposed to do? God was still first in my life, though.

Kiki spent the entire two-hour flight to Port Elizabeth talking about her cameras and various shoots she had experienced. It was so fascinating, and I listened in awe, even when I had no idea about what gadget or accessory she spoke. She was very experienced in her field as a freelance photographer and highly sought after. She had been a journalist like me before delving into the field of photography.

I knew Rodger had deliberately put me with her so that she could help me and guide me. I knew I'd learn more from her than what any book could teach me, and I knew I had to use this time very wisely. Trying to control my excitement and concentrate was the hardest part.

We were up at the crack of dawn, the hotel restaurant had just opened for breakfast, and we were the first ones there and helped ourselves to bottomless coffee and a healthy breakfast. Kiki warned me to stay away from the oily foods, as it might be possible that things would get out of control, and it could turn to bloodshed, and I'd probably lose all the food rather embarrassingly. I wasn't sure if she was joking or serious, but I stuck to the non-oily healthy food, and it was all still delicious.

We were the first journalists on the scene thanks to Rodger's informant and were allowed into the prison once we had shown our media passes.

Kiki knew exactly where the best position would be, on the wall just left of the main entrance gate, and it was as though she played this role on a daily basis. Which I suppose she did.

On the way there I tagged along behind her, asking relevant questions to anyone that looked like they might give me an answer. I got a few very good quotes from several people in the know. My Dictaphone was kept on, and I checked that I had brought the spare batteries quickly, as the thought of it going apartment during an important interview left me sweating.

Kiki laughed at me, 'You're doing fine, and I have plenty of spare batteries in all shapes and sizes. Just follow my lead.'

'Thanks, Kiki, my heart is going crazy from all this adrenaline.'

We waited a few minutes longer, and then the mass of prisoners came streaming into the courtyard towards the main entrance where we stood; Kiki was so right; this was the best position to be in. She had an incredible view for her lenses to capture the scene, all the facial expressions of the people on both sides of the fence.

The mass of prisoners came upon us like a swarm of bees, shouting, singing and waving banners and other objects. It was intimidating, and I was scared out of my boots, so much so that my hands began to shake. Kiki's camera was on a rampage clicking the shutter open and closed as fast as her fingers humanly could.

The wardens stood at their posts with their guns ready and loaded, all they needed was the signal to fire.

'You see that man there with the grey jacket?'

She pointed to a man on the right side of the huge entrance gates with a walkie-talkie radio in his hand.

'Go and speak to him.'

Without hesitation, I jumped down from the top of the wall where we had a bird's eye view of the entire scene and walked gingerly toward him.

He looked at me with such fierce intent I almost turned around and fled.

'Yes lady?' he said.

'I'm from the press. Could I ask you a few questions, please?'

He ushered me to the wall, saying, 'You got ten minutes.'

I fired my questions at him, having to yell above the noise from the prisoners who were now hovering five meters from where I stood. He spoke directly into my Dictaphone, giving me clear and precise answers. It was the best interview so far, and I'd thought he was no one in particular.

How had Kiki known he would be good to interview?

I needed to learn so much from her.

By lunchtime the prisoners were still chanting and threatening all sorts, a few prisoners had thrown objects about, but it had not yet become so violent that the wardens had to resort to firing any weapons. The officials and all the necessary, important people were behind closed doors bashing out the pros and cons of the prisoners' demands. The visiting dignitaries had been ushered out of the buildings not too long ago. Kiki must have captured some really good photos of them.

'Kaye, stand by the gate, front and center, quickly!'

I did as she told me. Again she was spot on, a spokesperson for the prison came out to address the press while the wardens went to speak to the large crowd of prisoners. There were prisoners yelling obscenities from windows above the courtyard encouraging those below to resort to extreme violence. As the mass of people cheered and sang out in a loud union of rejoicing, I strained to hear what the spokesperson was saying, but I had the Dictaphone right by his mouth. I was sure I got every word.

On my way back to Kiki I spoke to the man with the walkie-talkie once more. He was less intense as the negotiations seemed to have gone smoothly. He spoke freely while his deep baritone voice boomed above the noise.

The blood pumped wildly through my arteries; I was shaking, I was smiling non-stop, my eyes were as wide as saucers, completely and utterly exhilarated by the entire happenings of the day and the outcome.

It was my turn to talk non-stop to Kiki on the flight back. I had one question after another. 'How would I do this and how would I do that? How did you know that man would be so accommodating? How did you know they would go to the gate at that moment to speak to the press? Did you see the anger and violent expressions on their faces? How loud did they shout? I was so scared at one stage.'

I just couldn't shut up, poor Kiki was exhausted and tolerated me kindly, and I'm sure Rodger would hear all about my performance from her. He would certainly hear all about it from me, from the moment the plane lifted off to when I landed back in Durban.

What a rush it had been!

Chapter Twenty-Three

My article was a success and Rodger, a podgy man with a mop of grey hair and stress lines that encased his face, sent me on more and more assignments, almost always partnering me up with Kiki. The times that I had to go out with another photographer, the intensity was never that high nor the camaraderie. There was nothing wrong with their expertise or their devotion to their job, but Kiki just brought something extra to the table. She somehow managed to bring the best out in me too.

I was a little miffed at Spencer's lack of enthusiasm about my first breakthrough story. I had come home on such a high, super excited to tell him all about the weekend – the flight, the prisoners, the wardens, the interviews, everything!

All he wanted to know was, 'Were you in any danger?'

'No, Kiki knew where to be to get the best view and to be safest, but Spencer, it was so exhilarating!'

'Well as long as you weren't in any danger. I worked non-stop the whole weekend.'

And that was as interested as he was in the highlight of my career thus far.

When I had to go away for assignments, his only concern was if I would be in danger, and I felt that even then he asked out of habit more than actual concern.

His hours became increasingly long, and our intimacy and romantic life seemed to get confined to weekends; I hardly ever saw him during the week. Sometimes when he came home, I was already sleeping, and he would be gone when I woke up in the mornings. The evenings we were home together were spent in the study while we both worked.

He missed most Bible studies, but I went by myself rather than sit around waiting for him to get home. He did still make it to church on Sundays where he was as charming and friendly as ever. No one other than Evelyn would have guessed we lived such career-oriented lives.

I loved Sundays.

I worried that this marriage was not what God wanted it to be. It had been perfect when we'd found each other, and all the dots had dotted together to bring us as one before God, but our careers seemed to have taken precedence over our marriage.

I spoke to Spencer one day after a riveting sermon from Minister Lyle.

'We seem to be drifting away from God in our marriage, don't you think? I mean we used to pray together and talk about our spiritual lives all the time...' I trailed off.

'It's okay; we are fine. I know we don't pray together, but I do pray by myself and so do you. A lot of Christians have careers as we do. It's okay love, this will not last forever, and soon it will be five years, and we can start our family, and everything will be perfect.'

He wrapped his arms around me and cuddled me into his chest.

'I love you,' he mumbled as he kissed me wantingly.

His kiss still, after all, this time, did not melt me into nothing, but I guessed that only happened once in a lifetime and I'd had my chance of that.

I desperately prayed that God would continue to guide me and to help Spencer and me find our way back to being the committed Christian couple that we'd been when we'd married.

Saturdays with Evelyn remained our "get the load off your chest" dates. I poured my heart out to her about my marriage and where it stood with God.

'Don't be so hard on yourself, Kaye. God knows your heart; He knows you want it to be a perfect marriage. Just keep giving your marriage to God, and remember it will only work if you are both willing to give God a hundred percent.'

'That's what worries me. I don't think Spencer, and I are on the same page anymore.'

I felt my throat choke up with the horrible sentiments of disappointment.

After an exhausting day of meetings and deadlines and a very irritated boss, I packed up my bags and headed for my car that parked in the staff parking area.

I stood by the driver's door fiddling with the key, trying to get it into the lock of the door while trying to hold my handbag and my extra bag that held all my files, all at the same time.

'Hello,' said that familiar voice I knew so well, I was sure it was that voice, and I froze instantly.

I opened the door already starting to shake and a cold chill passed over me. I managed to throw my bags and files onto the driver's seat without everything falling out onto the asphalt or the floor of the car. Slowly I turned around, my heart beating so hard I couldn't hear myself think.

'You left.'

That was all I could muster as I stared at Boyd standing before me. I did not want to believe my eyes; I never thought I would ever see him again.

'Kaye, hello,' he said again, moving very slowly and gingerly towards me, 'how you keeping?'

'I...I...You left.'

Other words eluded me. I stared at him; my mouth was surely hanging on the floor.

'Kaye, I am so sorry, I can't explain why I did what I did. I just want to say sorry.'

He stood next to me and leaned against the side of my car. I took a step backward; I knew I should not stand too close to him. My brain started to dig up the anger and resentment and the pain that it had filed away, but my heart was yearning to reach out to him and hold him and to forgive him.

My brain won the battle for now.

'Why are you here? What do you want from me now, after all, this time?'

'I just want your forgiveness.'

I wasn't going to answer him. I tried, but my brain and my heart were in such a raging battle it left me trembling and fighting back the tears that rolled down my face uncontrollably.

'I can't speak to you now,' I said as I jumped into the car and battled to start it let alone put it into reverse then change gears into first and drive off.

Why has he come back?

Why do I still feel like I love him?

Why did you leave Boyd?

Why? Why? Why?

All the questions I asked had no answers and having no answers brought no rest to my mind at all. I became frantic almost to the point of a breakdown.

I pondered whether I should tell Spencer. I would probably not see Boyd again. But what if he told someone that he had seen me? They would surely tell someone else, and then the news would get back to Spencer. So I figured it was best to tell him before the people of the small community told him for me.

What did I have to fear? Boyd popped up out of nowhere and had unsettled me which was understandable. Spencer was my husband and deserved my honesty. I had just been complaining to Evelyn about our marriage not being what God would want it to be, and here I was contemplating keeping secrets from my husband. I reprimanded myself fiercely and prepared myself to tell Spencer when he got home.

It was a restless evening as I waited for Spencer. As the minutes ticked away, my head was bombarded with the image of Boyd leaning against my car, with a hardened yet emotionally broken expression on his face. He looked so much older, so haggard and he was tanned, or rather he had the army tan – his neck and arms were tanned.

I waited and waited and waited until Spencer got home from work. He hated it if I phoned his office as it always distracted his train of thought.

The more confused I became as to why Boyd would appear as an apparition, the more the anger surfaced, and I had to control the urge to phone his parents' house. Mrs. Langford was probably hysterical with happiness to see her beloved son again.

I was exhausted from all the endless thinking and reasoning that I eventually passed out on the couch. At eleven o'clock I woke up realizing that Spencer was still not home. He was never this late, so I made the call to his office.

No one answered – and I went to bed, falling asleep while praying God would guide me. Spencer would be home soon, and I would tell him in the morning.

Boyd filled my dreams, and I was restless all night.

When I woke up, I rolled over and reached for Spencer next to me. He wasn't there, but I could see he had slept there as the pillows were all scrunched from the indentation of his head. I looked all over the apartment to see if he was there but to no avail; he had already left.

I would have to wait until the evening tell him now, but how would I make it through the day with this running through my head?

When I got to work, I parked in my usual parking space and looked nervously around for Boyd, worrying that he would come back to try and speak to me again.

The office was a hive of activity for which I was very grateful; it took the constant worry of Boyd off my mind. While everyone slowed down for their lunch break, I made a phone call to Evelyn. I had to tell someone.

She was so shocked.

'What? What did he want?'

I tried to tell her what I remembered he had said; my head was still so fuzzy from the shock it was difficult to think of it all.

'Have you told Spencer?'

'I waited up for him last night but fell asleep before he came home, and then I wanted to tell him this morning, but he'd left before I woke up. I can't tell him this over the phone, so I will have to tell him tonight.'

'You must before he hears it from the grapevine!'

'Yes, that's what worrying me. I still don't get why he had to come and see me and was that it? Say hello and please forgive me, and that's it? I just can't understand it.'

'Kaye, I don't know what to say, this is so weird, and I can understand how confused you must be. You mustn't let Boyd get to you. He had his chance with you and blew it in the worst possible way.'

'I know you're right. Thanks, Evelyn. So good that I can always count on you.'

'You can always count on God and then me,' she corrected me before we ended our call.

Spencer for once was at home before I was.

'Good, now I can tell him,' I whispered to myself as I threw my keys into the bowl that stood on an oak table against the wall in the entrance way.

Then I walked straight into the kitchen where Spencer was standing in front of the kettle watching it boil.

'Hello,' I said going up to him to kiss him, 'I have something I must tell you.'

He looked at me, and I had not seen a look like that on his face ever before.

'Why didn't you tell me you saw Boyd?'

'I tried to! I waited up for you last night, and you left early this morning! I even tried to phone you at your office, but you never answered. How did you find out?'

'Evelyn told me,' he said, pouring the boiling water into our cups.

'When did you speak to Evelyn?' I was surprised, and it showed.

'Uhmm...She, hmm, she phoned me about the fellowship potluck on Sunday, and she let it slip.'

He put milk into the cups.

'He was in the parking lot of work waiting for me! He said hello and asked for my forgiveness, and I can't remember what all he said, but then I left. I wanted to tell you first, and I'm sorry you heard it from Evelyn instead.'

'If that man comes near you, I will; I will seriously hurt him, I promise you, Kaye. I don't care how big a crack shot he is; I will take him out.'

I was so astonished by his anger and his jealousy, he was red in the face, and his features were as hard as a stone.

'Spencer, he won't come back, I'm sure of it. He no doubt knows I'm married to you, and he got the message very clearly that I was not impressed with him. Can we please just put this behind us now?'

He left the kitchen and went out onto the balcony. I turned and looked into the sink and felt so sad. What did Boyd want by coming back and why did Spencer get so angry? It was not my fault I hadn't told him; I'd tried.

When Spencer finally came walking back into the kitchen, I was almost on the brink of tears, staring into the drain wondering if it could suck me in and carry me down the pipe.

'I'm sorry Kaye. I know it was Boyd's fault. I'm sorry I yelled at you.'

He stood behind me, put his arms around me and kissed my neck.

'It's just that he was your first love, and that is always a threat to any man.'

I turned around to face him, looked at him, at his piercing blue eyes, blinking the tears back from my own. He wiped them away gently with his thumbs while he held my face in his hands.

'I married you.'

'Yes, you did Mrs. Reed. I'm sorry. It wasn't your fault you couldn't tell me; I'm sorry I worked so late. Let's sit on the balcony and then please tell me all about it.'

'As long as you don't get angry again, Mr. Reed,' I smiled and let him take my hand leading the way to the balcony.

Explaining what had happened bolstered those confused fears and speaking about Boyd in front of Spencer I had a hard time keeping them in check. When I finished with the details of the Boyd episode, Spencer picked up my hands, held them in his and lifted them to his lips and kissed them.

'This Boyd must have had a screw loose to let you go, but I am not complaining,' he smiled, easing my very confused heart.

Perhaps this threat, if it could be called that, might just be the medicine our ailing marriage needed.

Had God sent us a warning sign?

Chapter Twenty-Four

I battled to shake the image of Boyd's face from my mind. It made me question whether I had ever got over him. I leaned heavily on God to banish the hold that Boyd had on my thoughts. I had forgiven him; I had moved on, I had forgotten him!

My phone rang at my desk and while typing my latest piece for the newspaper I reached for the receiver with my left hand knocking my half-full glass of water all over my legs while springing up out of the chair and answering the phone at the same time.

'Hello?' I squawked.

'Kaye. Please don't hang up.'

I was so tempted to throw the phone down and run. My hand immediately started shaking, and I gripped the receiver tightly causing my knuckles to whiten from the pressure. I sank back into my chair.

'What do you want?'

'I just want to hear you have forgiven me. I hate myself for what I did.'

'You do? Well, thank goodness for small mercies then.'

'Please Kaye, please forgive me.'

His pleading squished my heart into mush. I wanted him to hold me like he used to before the army.

The army! The army! How I hated the army.

'I forgave you a long time ago, and I've moved on, I'm married now in case you did not know.'

'Yes, my mom told me. Thank you, Kaye, I know I don't deserve it.'

'Everyone deserves forgiveness.'

Even though I sounded convinced, inside, I was crumbling.

'God, please keep me strong,' I silently asked.

'How are you? You happy?'

'Of course, I am! What kind of a question is that?'

'That's good.'

'Are you still in the army?' I asked, curiosity getting the better of me when I knew I should just end the call.

'Yes. I'm only home for a few weeks.'

A few weeks that would mean I might bump into him somewhere. My heart pumped madly.

'Well, I'm sure your parents are happy.'

'It's very strained, they have still not accepted my career choice, but yes, home is always home.'

I had to force the choked bubble in my throat to stay down. I began to fret as I clung to the phone. His voice was still Boyd's, and yet I could hear a saddened tone lingering on his lips.

His lips, his kiss. I wanted to kiss him, kiss those lips that could make me melt in a millisecond.

I rubbed my forehead with my free hand, trying to straighten out my brain, trying to rub out the thoughts that should not be there; they needed to disappear.

'Please give your family my regards. I have to go.'

'Okay, thanks again, Kaye. I hope I can say hello to you if we bump into each other while I am here.'

'Oh goodness – no please, I can't count on my reaction,' I wanted to say to him but said it to myself instead.

'Bye Boyd.'

I put the phone down for the sake of my sanity. Then I held my head in my hands, my elbows on the desk holding me up.

I prayed, 'Oh Lord, please forgive me for being so weak. I was so sure I had gotten over him. Please let us not bump into each other. Please Lord, please give me strength.'

I got up and went to the ladies' room, washed my face and stared in the mirror grateful that no one else was there.

Then I gave myself a pep talk, 'You in the mirror, get over it. You cannot allow Boyd to get to you like this. You are married. You love Spencer. Grow up! Let Jesus control you – not you!'

I scolded myself for ages, and when finally I was no longer alone in the ladies' room, I left.

I had fifteen minutes left to finish my article before the deadline. I had to concentrate. I had to forget Boyd and his phone call.

Before leaving the office I thought of phoning Evelyn to give her the whole sorry story, but then I remembered she'd let it slip the last time, and I decided against it.

Spencer had been far more loving, although he still worked such long hours, he wasn't so moody and short toward me since the Boyd episode. Today's little episode would surely upset the apple cart, so it was probably best left unsaid I decided.

I felt as though I was cheating on Spencer. We had always been honest with each other, but how could I explain this to him rationally when I couldn't react rationally myself?

And after his outburst the previous time, this time, he would surely go looking for Boyd and cause him bodily harm. I knew my decision was probably the wrong one, but I made it and prayed that God would forgive me for keeping secrets.

'You okay to go on an assignment in Pretoria for a few days?' Rodger interrupted my thoughts as if on cue.

'Yes, of course. What's the story?'

'My little birdie has told me that a very important diplomat will be in the country for secret behind-closed-doors talks with the prime minister. My little birdie is also setting up a secret behind-closed-doors interview for me.'

He smiled smugly and looked very proud of his little birdie.

'Do I ever get to meet this "little birdie"?' I laughed back at him.

'Never. You leave tomorrow.'

He gave me a thumbs up, turned and left.

I let out a heavy sigh, I was so grateful, more grateful than Rodger or his "little birdie" could ever imagine. Being on an assignment meant that I would not be in town. Not being in town meant that I had no chance of bumping into Boyd.

'Thank you, Lord.'

I looked upward and closed my eyes in sincere gratitude to God.

I dialed Spencer's office number. If he was working late again, there was the possibility that I would not see him before I left.

'Hi, how is your day going?' I asked first so his reply would set the tone for the rest of the conversation.

'Better than most days today. What's up?'

'I have to go away for a few days. I leave early tomorrow morning for Pretoria. Are you working late?'

'Is it going to be dangerous?'

His first reaction every time. I should have expected his reply.

'No. It's an interview with a diplomat, but I have to hang around to get the interview, it's not a definite time or date.'

'Okay. I won't be late tonight. See you later.'

'Okay, bye.'

We spent a wonderful evening together, one that we had not had for a very long time. Spencer took me to a quaint restaurant on the beachfront in Durban, and we devoured our steaks and sipped on red wine, all the while looking out over the ocean with the bright full moon and the light it cast on the waters. It was peaceful, and it was romantic.

How badly I'd needed an evening like this after that phone call. While watching a seagull fly through the moon-lit sky, I was filled with gratitude.

'Thank you, Lord, for putting me and my stupid failing heart in perspective,' I prayed silently.

For the first time since we had made the spare room into a study, we did not enter it that evening. At first, it was strange, the feeling that there was something we had to do lingered. But instead of heeding to it, we snuggled on the couch and watched a documentary on the TV.

When the show was over Spencer stood up, pulled me off the chair by my hands and led me to our bedroom.

How much I needed to be loved by him that night, he would never know, he would never have understood.

Chapter Twenty-Five

For two days while waiting for the interview, I had been sitting around, either in the hotel lobby or my hotel room. I was bored stiff of watching the guests check in or out at the reception desk, of the staff going about their duties and of the uninteresting documentaries they had on the TV channels, and I was, even more, bored of the hotel room. The green covers on the bed and cream colored walls did little to interest me. I was even sick of coffee.

Spencer phoned my room in the evenings when he got home from work, so during the day, I made the odd call to Evelyn or the office. Other than that there was nothing for me to do. I did not attempt to venture far from the hotel just in case the interview was going to happen.

While flipping through the selection of three channels, I phoned Evelyn.

'Hello,' she answered in an off tone, it sounded almost as though she had choked on her words while taking a breath of air at the same time.

'Hi, are you okay?'

'Oh I'm okay I suppose. Sian broke up with me this afternoon.' She sniffed a little as if stifling her tears.

'Oh, my friend! I'm so sorry, did he say why?'

'He wants his freedom and says he doesn't love me. The Strange thing is that we never once mentioned love. Well, there is not much I can do about, is there? I will survive I'm sure.'

'I wish I was there to give you a big hug.'

I had never really liked Sian. Evelyn needed someone who was equally intelligent, and that could balance her passion for God and her vivaciousness. Sian was cynical and sarcastic and found fault with everyone and everything. Still, I felt bad for my friend.

The third day of sitting in the Carlton Hotel and whiling the time away in the brightly lit restaurant having a chicken salad, a waiter arrived with a message written on the hotel's very fine stationery.

I thanked him and read it: *Meeting – four o'clock at attorney's chambers. Good luck.*

At last, the meeting was to go ahead! I pulled out my notebook and quickly scribbled down a few more relevant questions I might ask in the interview and jotted down suggestions and points to remember. Nervous and excited I rushed off to my room to prepare myself.

I got dressed very smartly, or as smartly as I could afford, in a black pants suit with a pale blue shirt. I pulled my hair back into a soft ponytail and applied a little basic makeup. All I needed was to look professional.

The reception room of the attorney's office was cold and unfriendly. The walls decorated with a few ugly landscape paintings that were un-colorful and boring, perfectly matching the boring brown chairs and carpet.

The receptionist scared me like no one ever had. She glared at me through her teardrop glasses that were at the tip of her long pointed nose and looked as though they were about to fall off. I got the instinctive feeling that she was not impressed that I had an interview arranged without her permission.

Her dark blue powdered eyes pierced my core with spits of fire as she told me to sit and wait in a gruff voice that I presumed she had inherited from all the cigarettes she smoked. The ashtray next to her typewriter was the evidence – it was overflowing with stubs and old ash.

With her very long painted, bony fingernails, she reached toward the keys of the typewriter to untangle a few, and her glasses slipped even further down her nose. Her grey hair was pulled back tightly in a small bun on the top of her head. I tried not to look at her, but she reminded me so much of a cartoon character, one that was always the evil old lady.

'You may go in,' she said to me, exposing her yellow stained teeth.

I gathered my bag and notepad in a flash and made for the door.

As I put my hand on the doorknob, she said, 'Sign here.'

I turned to see she had whizzed the duplicate paper from her typewriter and placed it on the table with a pen.

'What is it that I am signing?' I asked, keeping my distance for fear of attack.

'Just that you will not use the contents of the interview for your personal gain. Sign there.'

She pointed to the dotted line at the bottom of the page. I glanced through the contents of the one-page agreement and signed it, taking the duplicate copy with me and then I made for the door. I opened it cautiously as a very tall, smartly dressed, over-cologned, bald man approached me with his hand extended revealing an expensive gold watch.

'Mrs. Reed welcome, I am Mr. Jordine, and this is my client Mr. Juback.'

'Thank you for this opportunity,' I said, nervously sitting down in the chair alongside Mr. Juback, and at the opposite end of Mr. Jordine's very large dark wooden desk.

His office was large and bragged of his achievements and qualifications all over the walls. There were also photos of him with very influential and famous people, obviously meant to impress prospective clients.

'Shall I get Mrs. Archibald to organize coffee?'

He looked at me for a response.

'No,' I blurted out and then had to recover, 'I mean no thank you, I have had more than enough coffee, thanks.'

Mr. Jordine couldn't stifle the giggle that slipped through his shiny white teeth.

'Mrs. Archibald is scary, but she looks after me better than anyone, and I trust her with my life.'

I believed him; no one would dare go near him as long as she was around. He sat behind his desk lighting up a cigarette and immediately I felt like coughing, the image of my parents floated to the surface of my mind unwillingly.

'You may go ahead,' he said and pointed to Mr. Juback with his large fat fingers decorated with an array of gold rings.

Mr. Juback turned toward me in acknowledgment and approval. He looked tired; dark rings circled his eyes. He too was dressed in expensive clothing, and if he was wearing any cologne, it made no impact as Mr. Jordine's overpowered it. He was of average height but grossly overweight that it made him appear a lot shorter than he was.

He was gracious with his replies but very secretive, and I had to ask him the same question several times trying various angles. I had to drag the truth from him.

I asked simple questions such as, 'Are you satisfied with the outcome of the hearing? Did you have a successful meeting with the prime minister? Were you aware that if you came forward, he would pardon your brother? Why did it take you so long to come forward with this information? Have you seen your brother in prison since you arrived in South Africa? How is your relationship with your brother now? Will you wait for him to be released and return home to Egypt with him or not?'

After three hours I finally felt I had extracted everything possible from Mr. Juback. It was not only my questioning that took so long, but Mr. Jordine also took it upon himself to answer on behalf of Mr. Juback, and at times they conversed with each other in their native tongue; and that I found extremely rude.

I opened Mr. Jordine's office door very slowly and was so relieved that Mrs. Archibald was no longer at her desk, and I would never have the displeasure of crossing her path ever again.

After a shower and dinner in my room, I finalized the article so that in the morning I could type it out and give it to Rodger the moment he walked into the office. I finished at about ten o'clock and since Spencer had not yet called I dialed our home number. There was no reply. I dialed his office number and got no response there either. Perhaps he was on his way home, and he would call soon.

I lay back on the bed, resting my papers on my lap and allowed the puffy pillows to swallow my head. If Spencer phoned me when he got home, I had no idea as I was asleep almost instantly.

Chapter Twenty-Six

The published article received excellent recognition on Monday morning. My first front page news and I had to admit to myself that I was very proud of it, and my first reaction was to tell Spencer.

'You must buy the paper! I got the front page.'

'Okay I will later, well done,' he replied in an apartment tone that rather hurt me as I was hoping he would, at least, be excited for me.

Perhaps he had people in his office and was not able to be more expressive. I hoped that was the case when I hung up the phone.

Rodger stood next to my desk holding an envelope out to me.

'For you, but you not to tell anyone.'

I looked up at him confused as even he seemed to be acting strangely.

'What's this?'

'Open it later, not here.'

'Uhm, okay, must I say thanks or should I start to cry?' I gave a curious smile.

He laughed at me and walked away.

I turned the envelope around inspecting it for any clues and feeling the contents trying to make out what it was. I felt a pang of despair as this envelope reminded me of Boyd's letter. Shaking my head at the idea that the contents would be similar, I got up and made my way to my car, I had to know what it was.

I took a drive to Inyoni Rocks and parked facing the ocean, and while still in my car I opened the envelope.

'Oh, my word!' I exclaimed out loud.

There was a note and one hundred Rand in cash.

It read: *Well done on an excellent bit of journalism. Mr. Juback was very impressed with you I'm told. Enjoy the bonus.*

I was so flabbergasted and examined the note over and over thinking all the time what I would spend it on.

Spencer was home early thank goodness, as my excitement was almost running out of the door by now. With the envelope in my hand, I held it out toward him as he put his briefcase down on the chair in the study. He looked at me through his tired eyes; that blue piercing color seemed dull and yet as he gazed upon my smile the brightness slowly returned. My excitement seemed to be contagious; I hoped it was.

He took it with a sigh and opened it slowly. I could see his expression lift as he pulled the money out, stretching it with his long fingers.

'And this?' he asked, finally cracking a smile.

'Read the note.'

I pointed to it, the smile still stuck on my face, I felt like a little girl revealing a big surprise from Santa. He opened the letter slowly still holding the money, took two steps toward me and put his arms around me.

'Well done Kaye,' he said softly then gave me a gentle kiss.

He put the money and the note back in the envelope and gave it back to me.

'Really Kaye, well done.'

I was too happy to care about his lack of enthusiasm.

'I'm going to use it for a weekend away for us, somewhere peaceful.'

'When?'

'I don't know yet; tomorrow I will make a few phone calls.'

'Uhm, perhaps not just yet. Can it wait till we take our leave?'

'But that's months away still, we could use a mini break now.'

'No, not now, when we take our leave, Kaye.'

His voice was stern and short, and I knew better than to argue the point, as by now I was used to this tone of voice which meant it was the end of the conversation.

I was despondent, even though he was tired and stressed with his workload he was unable to be enthusiastic with me. He knew a mini-break would be ideal for both of us; we had discussed it a few times already.

I walked out of the study to the bedroom and put the envelope in my bag. Spencer made no attempt to follow me but instead opened his briefcase and took out the work he had brought home. Then I went to the kitchen and started preparing dinner.

While going through the motions of making a meal of macaroni and cheese, I tried to figure out why Spencer had become so distant. It wasn't his workload I was sure of it, when he was at the church he was cheerful and almost his normal self – or was that also an act?

When the meal was ready, I called out to Spencer to come and eat. There was no reply, and so I called out to him again, still no reply. I took the short walk from the kitchen past the small dining area and then the living room and almost immediately turned right into the study. My heart skipped a beat as I saw Spencer sitting in his chair with his head on his folded arms on the desk, resting on all his papers. I had never seen him fall asleep over his papers like this before, definitely not so early in the evening.

I tip-toed lightly over the carpet until I was at his side and gently touched his shoulder.

'Spencer, hey Spencer!'

He lifted his head up slowly, probably confused and surprised that he had fallen asleep.

'What, oh wow did I fall asleep?'

'Yep, seems like it. You haven't done that before; you must be really tired. Get into bed,' I said lovingly stroking his hair that had fallen forward.

'Suppose I should hey.'

He stood up gradually and without moving his papers back into order side-stepped me and made his way to our bedroom. He changed his clothes and flopped on the bed, asleep within seconds.

I went back to the kitchen, dished up a plate of food for myself and made my way to the couch. I felt awfully guilty that my only concerned was for my feelings; I should have realized he was beyond tired.

Before I got stuck into my food – I was really hungry – I prayed the Lord bless it to my body and for Him to be with Spencer and me, for Him to bring us both back to be the servants we had promised to be.

It worried me so much that we were allowing our careers to become more important than God in our lives. Spencer always convinced me that we would only be this busy for the next few years.

'Remember our five-year plan, and then it will all be better,' he would say whenever I mentioned it to him.

I had to believe this was acceptable to God, although deep inside I knew it wasn't.

When I woke up in the morning, Spencer had already left. He hadn't stirred when I'd eventually got into bed the previous night. He must have been completely exhausted, and I felt immensely sorry for him.

In the office, once I settled for the day, I phoned Evelyn, knowing she was at home without any classes this morning.

'Hi, how are you?' I asked in my usual friendly greeting voice.

'Kaye, hi.'

She seemed surprised to hear my voice even though she knew I would call today as I did every Friday morning.

'So where we meeting tomorrow?' I asked.

'Oh I, I don't think I can make it tomorrow.'

Her voice was hesitant, and she replied as if she had to choose her words carefully.

'Why not? We've never missed a Saturday unless I've been away.'

'I have some serious studying to do.'

'I thought your exams were still a few months away?'

'They are, but I have fallen behind, and I need to catch up somehow. I'm sorry Kaye.'

When I put the receiver down, I accepted her excuse. Who was I to argue with her? If she had to study that was her priority.

Spencer was working as usual, and so for the first time in a very long time, I was alone on a Saturday morning and at home without any plans.

What would I do?

I found myself at Baggies. It had been absolute ages since I had been there; actually, I could not remember being there since the wedding.

The feel of the sand between my toes as I made my way to the ocean with my board under my arm brought back a wave of emotions, memories and a longing I had forgotten.

Had I missed this so much and not even realized it?

I sat on my board bobbing up and down waiting for a wave that was decent, or perhaps it wasn't that I was waiting for a wave, it was more like just wanting to sit out there in the water and have time to refocus my life. Perhaps Spencer and Evelyn not being around this morning and giving me the chance to get myself back in the ocean was God at work. He wanted me to reflect on my life and possibly where it was headed.

Was Spencer correct when he always said that God would understand that we had a five-year plan? I wondered by whose terms we lived – ours or God's. Who was in control of our lives – us or God?

I spent ages simply sitting on my board, floating over some possibly good rideable waves while I pondered over issues. By the time, I realized I was the only one left out there in the mass of blue water I finally caught a small wave to the shore. I dried off, made use of the café for something to eat and sat at one of the tables while I ate. I noticed so many new faces hanging around and realized that to them I must look like one of the old people; they were now the "in crowd" and they still had the world at their fingertips. Oh, where had those carefree days gone when all we wanted to do was surf at Baggies?

'Hi Kaye,' a familiar voice said, disturbing my train of thought.
'Rosalie hi. Gosh, I have not seen you for ages. Well, I haven't been here in ages I guess.'

She sat down with her food, and we chatted for a long time about our lives, about our wonderful school days and Boyd and York. I suddenly missed York so much, and at the same time, I was annoyed at him for leaving me just as Boyd had done. I wondered where Boyd was and what he was doing or if I would ever see either of them again; I wondered so many things.

The weather changed rapidly as it often did on the South Coast, but this time, we were in for a couple of days of heavy storms according to the weather forecast on the radio in my car.

Chapter Twenty-Seven

I bought a big slab of chocolate and went to Evelyn's apartment on my way home from Baggies. I was sure she would appreciate the gesture. I parked my car outside her building. The wind had picked up by now, and as I opened my car door it almost flew off its hinges – I just managed to grab it in time but too late to prevent the chocolate and my keys from falling out of my hand. When I had steadied the door with my one hand and collected my things in the other, I got out of the car. My hair, loose and still slightly wet from the sea, took off upward as I got out the car as the gusts of wind tossed it. I had to fight against the wind to close the door, hold the things in my hand and try to control my hair. Walking towards the building was a great effort as the corners of the building created swirling winds wanting to throw me off my feet. I was so grateful not to be wearing a skirt or a dress – it probably would've taken off with the skirt acting as a parachute.

When I eventually got to Evelyn's apartment, I knocked on her door, but there was no answer. I knew she was home as I had seen her car in her allotted parking spot. I knocked again, and there was still no answer, so I turned the bronze doorknob left, and the door edged inward. I opened the door just enough to let myself in and closed it behind me quietly.

'Evelyn!' I called out loud enough for her to hear me but not too loud that it would wake her up if she were sleeping.

There was still no answer, so I put the chocolate on the table by the door and went to her bedroom. Evelyn was lying curled up on her bed crying into her pillow. I rushed to her side, sat down next to her and put my arm over her back.

'Evelyn, what's wrong?'

She looked up at me, and I could tell she had been crying for a long time, her eyes were swollen and red. In fact, her whole face was swollen and red. She just shook her head and sobbed out loud, her body jolting as it expelled the air from within her.

I got up and hurriedly and put on the kettle. She needed something to calm her down, and I knew she always had hot chocolate in the cupboard, she always said it relaxed her. I rushed back to the room where she continued to wreak havoc on her pillow, and I sat next to her again putting my arms around her as best I could.

'What has happened, Evelyn?'

She awkwardly sat up, and after I handed her a couple of tissues, she wiped her eyes and blew her nose several times. She tried hard to stop herself from crying, but each time she tried to tell me what had upset her so much her emotions overcame her and wracking sobs escaped her. She sat on her bed, in a sorry mess, her pale blue skirt was wrinkled, and her red hair looked as though it had done an hour in the wind outside. Her dark eyes were blacker than usual.

While she went to the bathroom, I made her hot chocolate and found some cookies, put them on a plate for her and went back to the room. When she came out of the bathroom, I took her hand and led her back to the bed and helped her to sit down gently.

'Here is some hot chocolate and cookies for you,' I pointed to them, and she nodded.

Through her sobs and snorts, she managed to speak.

'I went to the doctor this morning,' she said as she took a deep shuddering breath before continuing, 'I'm…I…Kaye, I'm..oh Kaye...I'm pregnant!'

She burst out crying hysterically once more, throwing her arms around me hugging me, holding me with such force that I felt her body jerk with each and every sob and teardrop.

'Oh, Evelyn, oh, I am so sorry. Have you told Sian?'

I naturally presumed it was Sian's baby as she had not dated anyone since they had broken up and she did not do the one-night stand dates at all.

'No.'

'Have you told anyone?' I asked while she still held onto me desperately.

'My parents, this morning.'

I could feel the hysteria building up inside her again.

'They...Oh ...They are so furious.'

'I'm so sorry my friend.'

I did not know what else to say.

'When are you going to tell Sian?'

'No, not yet,' she said and burst into another round of hysteria, her tears rapidly descending her cheeks.

'You have to tell him, Evelyn. Why didn't you want to tell me earlier? You can't go through this alone.'

She didn't reply but instead held onto me as if I were the glue she needed to stick her back together. By the time she had calmed herself a little, it was almost dark outside; the storm was building up to be an epic one.

'Let me quickly phone Spencer and tell him I am staying here for a while longer.'

I got up to do what I intended.

'No don't,' Evelyn said hastily and grabbed my arm to stop me before I stood up fully, 'my parents will be here any minute, please stay here just until they come.'

'I will wait till they get here then and if you want me to stay longer, then I will.'

Evelyn lets her waterworks flow, and as I held her trembling body, comforting her, it reminded me of the many times she had done this same thing for me after Boyd had left. I was so grateful to be here for her in her time of need.

She had just finished her second cup of hot chocolate when we heard the door open, and slam shut not a few seconds later.

'You need to leave now Kaye, thank you,' her father said marching briskly into her bedroom. He was furious, the drive from Howick had not eased his fury at all.

I gave Evelyn a final hug and kissed her cheek gently; I could see the pain and fear in her eyes. I greeted her father as I walked passed him, who offered no response and passed her mother sitting on the couch. She, at least, said goodbye. I felt so sorry for my dear friend.

'Where have you been?' Spencer blurted out when I walked into our apartment windswept, and after putting my board back against the wall in the study, I replied.

'I went to Baggies, then to Evelyn. She is in some trouble…'

I was in the bathroom by now taking off my clothes and jumping into the shower.

'What trouble?'

He seemed frozen to the spot still in the living room which meant we were yelling at each other to get heard.

'Come here, and I will tell you!' I yelled back.

He came into the bathroom, pushed the toilet lid down and sat on it while I stood under the hot water of the shower.

'She is pregnant. I stayed with her until her parents got there. Her father is furious.'

I told him the events of my day from bobbing in the ocean to when I landed up at Evelyn. He never said a word but only listened.

After some time, he finally spoke, 'What is she going to do?'

'What do you mean by that?'

'I don't know really,' he spluttered, 'I mean she has to finish her degree, which is going to be difficult with a baby.'

'We couldn't talk about it; she was far too upset for that. I suppose her parents will discuss everything with her.'

'Oh right.'

He remained seated on the toilet while I went on describing what had happened between Evelyn and me without interruption. Spencer just sat on the toilet deep in thought and listened.

Much later in the evening, I dialed Evelyn's number at her apartment. I did not expect her to answer as her parents were probably still with her or she would be in a restless sleep from pure exhaustion. So I was surprised when she did, and by her voice, it was easy to tell that she was in fact very tired.

'Hi, how you?' I said into the receiver.

'Oh hi Kaye, I don't know right now.'

'Are your parents still there?'

'No, they've left, it was so horrible.'

She sniffed, trying very hard not to burst into tears all over again.

'Do you want me to come over?'

'No don't come over now, it's too late and besides this storm is crazy.'

'Try to get some sleep, and I will see you tomorrow then.'

She couldn't help the tears as we said goodbye and I would have to pray very hard for my dear friend tonight before I went to sleep.

It was strange that Evelyn had not yet told Sian she was pregnant. The more I tried to reason with her the more she put it off. Sian had moved to Johannesburg and occasionally phoned her, but the rest of us had not heard from him nor did we have any contact details for him and Evelyn was not sharing them with us either.

I worried about her, she had the worst case of morning sickness and still had to continue with her classes at the university. She was extremely irritable, understandably. Sometimes she was so ill she had to miss class for days which meant she always had catching up to do, as much as I wanted to, there was nothing I could do to help her.

Her parents had softened after the initial shock, and that was a blessing on its own. She would need her parents, especially her mother, and especially since there was not going to be a father around.

She had stopped going to church, and this worried me more than anything. I gathered she was ashamed and exhausted, and I constantly prayed that she would return to the kindest people in the world and not turn her back on God.

Minister Lyle offered to counsel with her, but she refused his offer. It was as though she was purposely cutting herself off from everyone. After Bible study one evening Minster Lyle asked me to stay behind for a few minutes. He asked after Evelyn, and I could not shed any more light on the situation than what he already knew. We prayed for her together; it was all we could do for her.

Our Saturday morning visits were automatically at Evelyn's apartment as she never wanted to go anywhere anymore. She said she hated the way people stared at her; she got enough of that at the University.

'I wonder what it's like to be pregnant,' I said to Spencer one Saturday afternoon.

He was working even more than usual if that was at all possible and so when he was home, we rarely did anything other than vegetating on the couch. He would force himself to come with me to church on Sundays.

'Don't even think about it Kaye,' he retorted.

'I did not say I want to be pregnant. I said I wondered what it felt like. There's a huge difference,' I snapped back defensively.

'Well, that's how it starts. First, you think about it, and then you start wanting it, and then it becomes an obsession,' he replied accusingly.

'And I suppose you are now talking from experience?'

He angered me when he scolded me as a father would his child. I was not his child. Before we got ourselves into a silly fight, I moved away from him and stood in the kitchen. I felt his arms move around my waist, and an apology whispered into my ear.

I turned around and looked into his blue eyes, 'I know we have our five-year plan. I have not forgotten.'

'I know, I'm sorry.'

He put his head down and looked at the white tiles on which we stood. I lifted his head so that he was looking at me again.

'I don't like the space we are in at the moment. I've told you this many times. We have such little time to spend together actually and those times I don't want to spend arguing, especially over something we both know is not going to happen.'

'I know, I'm sorry,' he said again and held me closer, kissing my forehead tenderly.

'Let's go out for dinner; we could both use a change of scenery.'

'Sounds like a plan,' Spencer uttered while he still hugged me in his embrace.

I relaxed, relishing his arms around me, a rather rare occurrence.

Chapter Twenty-Eight

The torrential subtropical rains had hit our little town in full force. We had days and days of endless rain without any signs of it easing in the near future. I was sick to death of frizzy hair and wet feet.

My usually neat and tidy cubical in which I worked in the large room filled with journalists and editors was drowning in papers. The screened cubical walls pinned with various articles I had published, various messages, and, even more, unfinished articles. My desk had papers everywhere – some falling out of their trays, some in little piles of their own and some were on the desk for reasons I still had to figure out. The wastepaper bin was full to the brim of scrunched up balls of paper. Story writing was not for the fainthearted.

I placed another piece of blank A4 paper into the typewriter – hopefully, I would get the story right this time – and let my fingers do their magic, having to stop every so often to unjam the keys as I typed faster than the machine could cope.

It was one of those days, and it was only ten in the morning. Engrossed in the words flowing from my brain to my fingers to the sheets of paper in the typewriter, lost to the world around me. When the phone rang, I got such a fright that I pushed down on several keys at once causing a huge congestion. Frustrated I answered on the third ring.

'Hello, Kaye speaking.'

'Good morning, am I speaking with Mrs. Reed?'

I could immediately hear it was a person in an official capacity.

'Yes, who am I speaking to?'

'I am Sister Goodwin from Addington Hospital. Your husband has been in an accident and admitted to ICU.'

I felt my heart collapse, pass through my knees and sink into the floor.

'I'll be there in a few minutes,' I said, already standing up from my chair and grabbing my bag.

The jammed typewriter and its story would have to wait. Scurrying passed Rodger's office I put my head in quickly.

'Spencer was involved in an accident, I'm going to the hospital, and I will phone you from there. Sorry, the story is not finished, the notes are on my desk, and I have most of it done. Can someone else finish it?'

I didn't wait for his answer.

The twenty-five-minute drive to the hospital took almost an hour in the pouring rain and heavy traffic. I must have passed at least three accidents on the way; this did not bode well with my nerves.

As I reached the nurses' station in the ICU ward, still taking off my jacket, the nurse ushered me into Spencer's room. I trembled when I saw how still he lay.

'Is he going to be okay?' I asked, finally allowing the tears to roll down my cheeks.

'The doctor will be with you shortly,' she said motioning for me to sit in the chair next to the bed and then she left me alone with him.

It was a dimly lit room, and the blue curtains were drawn, shutting out the faint light from the stormy skies outside. The bed was in the middle of the room against the wall on the left with just a single machine on the shelf above his head, monitoring his heartbeat. Another chair was standing in the middle of the wall opposite the entrance to the room; it looked sad and lost.

I took his hand; it felt warm but lifeless, and I shivered, and just then the doctor walked into the room.

'Mrs. Reed, I am Dr. Braun.'

He shook my shaking hand.

'Your husband looks worse than he is. From what I understand, he was hit on the side by another car, and he suffered a severe blow to the head. From the x-rays, there seems to be no serious damage, and he should come out of this state of unconsciousness soon. It might be today, or it might be in a few days but no longer than that. He needs to stay here in ICU until he wakes up.'

Dr. Braun smiled at me reassuringly, but he did not console me by any means. I stared at him trying to say something sensible.

Instead, he said, 'If there is anything you need to know, please ask the staff. If they can't assist you, they can phone me. You

are welcome to stay here with your husband until he wakes up.'
He smiled again.

'Thank you I will stay here,' I said and sat back in the chair still trembling.

I leaned on the bed holding Spencer's hand.

'Hey, it's me. Wake up please.'

Not so much as an eyelash flickered. I put my head on his hand and prayed.

'Is there someone we can contact for you?'

A nurse appeared at the door interrupting my prayer.

'Uhmm…Would you mind if I phone?'

She slowly walked with me to the nurses' station and passed the phone to me.

'Just dial zero to get a line,' she said and went on with her duties.

First I phoned Spencer's mother. His parents were in their late seventies and no longer able to travel. While I explained as best as possible that it was not serious, his mother remained unconvinced and distraught. I was afraid of what this news might do to his father's weak heart, and I felt bad that I'd phoned.

Rodger, he assured me that I could stay with Spencer as long as I needed to and that he'd found someone to finish the story. I felt a little sense of relief at that.

Then I phoned Evelyn hoping the news would not upset her and the baby too much.

'Oh no! Oh no! Oh no! Poor Spencer!'

Then she cried. Pregnancy made a woman far more emotional than usual, I surmised.

'He will be fine,' I tried to comfort Evelyn, 'the doctor said he must just wake up.'

'Are they sure? What if there is damage that they haven't picked up yet? Maybe the x-rays didn't show it.'

'You're scaring me, Evelyn. Don't talk like that. He will be fine; he has to be.'

'I'll be there in an hour,' she said and put the phone down.

What if the doctors were wrong as Evelyn suggested?

What if Spencer never woke up?

I felt like vomiting. A nurse came in to check Spencer's pulse and blood pressure.

'You look a little pale my dear. Just stay in that chair, and I'll be back with some cookies.'

She rushed out of the room and returned a few minutes later with a glass of orange juice and a plate of cookies. I thanked her feebly. I sipped at the juice and nibbled on the cookies all the while holding Spencer's hand, stroking his arm and talking to him. He didn't move for what seemed like hours.

In less than an hour, the nurse returned with Evelyn close on her heels.

'This lady says she is a close friend…' The nurse trailed off.

Evelyn didn't bother for me to answer or for the nurse to give her permission to come any closer, like a flash she brushed passed the nurse and threw her arms around me as I was standing up out of the chair. The nurse left us.

After embracing me with her now slightly enlarged tummy, she turned to Spencer and with one look burst into tears. She lifted his hand as I had done.

'Wake up Spence,' she whispered.

Evelyn pulled the sad chair up to the other side of the bed opposite me. Our hands were occupying both Spencer's hands.

We spoke to him; we stroked his arms. I wiped his face and ran my fingers around his eyes, down his cheeks, and over his lips praying all the while that my touch would awaken his senses and that he would open his eyes.

'Open your eyes, Spencer, open your eyes,' I pleaded – and Evelyn cried.

I returned from the fastest bathroom break of my life, to find Evelyn standing up leaning over Spencer, whispering to him. I approached the bed, touched by her concern for him, and held his hand again. Evelyn looked at me, tears streaming down her face – pregnancy did make women emotional it seemed!

I looked at Spencer's face and was not sure if I imagined it, but I was sure his eyelid had twitched.

'Watch his eyelid; I'm sure it moved.'

We both stared intently at his face.

Evelyn touched his eyelid softly with her index finger, and it positively moved this time. We both noticed it clearly. We waited a little longer to see if it would move again. I stroked his face and hair and stared at his face all the while. Both eyes twitched with definite movements this time.

'Quickly call the nurse,' I said to Evelyn, and she ran out of the room.

'Spencer, hey, can you hear me? It's me, can you hear me? Open your eyes.'

Evelyn and the nurse were both standing by the bed before I had finished my sentence. Evelyn picked up his hand again. The corners of his mouth twitched, and he mumbled, we were all sure of it.

'Spencer love, hey Spence, say that again. Open your eyes!' I pleaded.

His mouth moved as if he was trying to form a word and we all held our breath, his eyes flickered but not yet opening, and we all glanced at each other in anticipation. He was coming round. The nurse left to phone the doctor.

Spencer muttered something again.

'What was that you said, Spencer? Say it again.'

I leaned closer to his ear so that I could hear him. We watched him carefully; his lips moved to form words.

'Evelyn,' he said, clearly this time.

'What?' I said confused.

Why would he call her name first?

'Evelyn.'

He said it firmly and even more clearly than the first time.

'What?' I said a little louder.

Evelyn stood up straight and looked at me, her eyes as wide as saucers.

'Evelyn,' he said a third time and, this time, she leaned closer to him. I stood up straight and looked at them incredulously.

'I'm here,' she said rubbing her hand along his arm, 'I'm here.'

'Love you…The baby…'

'WHAT?' I asked very loudly.

I backed away from the bed confused and in utter disbelief at what I had just heard.

Had I misunderstood Evelyn's affection for him?

'Evelyn, what is going on here?' I looked at her with horror-stricken eyes.

Slowly she turned in my direction, not looking at me but toward me, her hands clutching her tummy.

'Evelyn!' I said harshly, forcing her eyes to look at me.

She looked up still clutching her tummy, her eyes brimming with tears.

'Oh, I'm so sorry Kaye, we never meant to…I...'

I didn't give her time to finish her sentence.

'WHAT ARE YOU TELLING ME?' I yelled.

Evelyn stared at the floor, her hand still resting on Spencer's arm.

'Are you telling me that you and Spencer, the baby? That it's Spencer's baby?'

I was shaking as I stuttered.

Evelyn stood rooted to the spot, and still looking at the floor she moved her head to look at him and then she nodded. She remained holding his hand tightly.

'OH MY WORD, HOW COULD YOU? HOW COULD YOU?' I screamed at her.

The nurses had by now all gathered in the room due to the commotion and were trying to find out what was going on.

'HOW COULD YOU?' I shouted at Evelyn, hysteria overcoming me.

I couldn't stop shouting the same question over and over again; I was so dreadfully shocked and confused. Evelyn just stood there by Spencer's side, tears streaming down her cheeks, one hand gripping his and the other supporting her baby.

I couldn't even look at Spencer. I turned and ran out of the room, down the corridor; ran down the four flights of stairs and out of the hospital entrance.

The rain slapped me in the face as I exited the building where I had entered as a different person, only a few hours before. I stopped and bent forward, resting my hands on my knees, battling to get my breathing under control. Between the lack of air from the running and the erratic breathing due to the shock of what I had just got confronted with, I struggled to find the correct rhythm to get sufficient air into my lungs. I stood up straight and looked at the sky, drenched; but somehow managed to at last regulate my breathing. Then I ran to a coffee shop in the building next to the hospital.

I was soaking wet, the few people that were in there already stared at me as I sat down at a table by the window that looked out onto the ocean, a pool of water already forming under my chair.

What had just happened?

A young lady came and got my order of coffee and as I stared out of the window the bad weather upgraded into a gale force storm.

Chapter Twenty-Nine

What was I going to do?

My husband and my best friend were lovers and in a few months were going to have a baby.

How had this happened?

Evelyn was such a strong Christian, and Spencer, although he put his work first, was too. Although, did he, in fact, work such long hours or had he always been at her place?

Was I being punished for putting our five-year plan before God? Ha! Our five-year plan – that was a joke. I wonder what plan he'd had with Evelyn.

I snickered in disgust at the thought of the fool I had been made out to be.

The elderly lady sitting next to me asked, 'Are you, alright dear?'

I moved my head just millimeters, enough so that I could see her from the corner of my eye. Her eyes were old and had lost a lot of the sparkle that shines with youth, but they looked at me with concern.

'I'm fine,' I replied bluntly and returned to gazing outside, sighing heavily.

'Oh Lord please help me. I don't understand why this has happened to me. Please help me,' I prayed silently, finally taking a sip of the coffee that had been standing in front of me for a while already.

It was almost cold, but I drank it nevertheless. My hands were shaking both from the shattering revelation and my wet clothes that stuck to me. The heat from the room and all the people in it had indeed warmed me up somewhat. However, my clothes were still soaked.

'That must be cold dear, let me get you another cup.'

I looked up as one of the gentlemen at the table spoke, and when I started to protest, he shushed me and somehow caught the attention of the waitress, ordering another cup of coffee for everyone at the table. The poor waitress fought her way through the people blocking every walking area there was, and had to do it again on her return this time with a decanter full of coffee. She refilled our cups with a smile and left.

'Thank you,' I said to the kind man.

'What brings you out in this weather?'

I suppose he thought to take this moment as a gap to strike up a conversation with me. My table guests looked at one another inquisitively. There was nothing more intriguing than a story you knew would be interesting if told. They all sensed that I had one of those stories, and I could see the curiosity in their eyes.

The storm was not going to abate soon, and I realized I had left my handbag and jacket in the hospital room. I had to go back there. My nerves fluttered through my veins at the thought of facing Spencer and Evelyn again.

What would I say or do?

How could they have deceived me so and worst of all how could they have deceived God?

I wanted to blurt out my sad and pathetic life story to these strangers, but what would that help? They would get a juicy story to tell their friends and families, and I would still have to face the same sordid hurt and pain.

I took out the ten cents I had in my pants pocket – a habit I always kept – and left it on the table for the first cup of coffee.

Whether I left now or later, the weather wasn't going to change, and I still had to face the two worst traitors I had ever known. I fought my way to the shop door, and with someone's help, I managed to open the door against the force of the wind. I then fought my way back to the hospital. The raindrops stung my face even though I was bent forward, battling to take a single step in the right direction. I felt like a drunk person staggering in the street.

I shook the water off my body like a dog when I entered the hospital foyer and slowly made my way to the ICU ward using the elevators this time.

As I approached the nurses' station, all the nurses stopped what they were doing and focused on me, clearly, they all knew my pathetic tale. The nurse that had attended to me when I had first arrived walked up to me and put her jersey over my shoulders.

I hadn't realized I was shivering; even my teeth were chattering together.

'Sit over here for a while and warm up first dear,' she said as she switched on a heater and dragged a chair in front of it.

I looked at her, questioning her motives.

Was she concerned or was she deliberately keeping me away from Spencer's room?

The other nurses joined her bringing me hot chocolate and cookies and towels to dry myself as much as possible. I had their sympathy, and they were in my corner there was no doubt about that.

'Is she still with him?' I asked through my chattering teeth.

'No. The doctor ordered her away; she is not family of his.'

I snorted, 'She's carrying his baby.'

The distaste rolled off my tongue like a plague.

'Mr. Reed came round, and there is no sign of any concern, but the doctor is keeping him here for two days for observation, and then he can go home.'

'Humph! Which home? Certainly not mine.'

They never replied. It was not their place to answer me, but I knew they felt my pain, it was written all over their faces.

When I felt better, I walked into the dimly lit room and observed Spencer sleeping in an almost sitting position. The single machine that was above his head removed. I carefully lifted my jacket from the chair, and as I picked up my bag, my keys rattled, waking him up.

'Kaye,' he said lifting his hand toward me.

'Are you sure you don't mean Evelyn?' I spat at him.

'Kaye – please – can we talk about this?'

'Talk, you want to talk to me about this?'

The anger that rose up inside me was new to me. I had never felt such a violent rage stir my actions. I felt I wanted to hit him back into unconsciousness. I wanted to gouge his eyes out. I wanted to hurt him so badly that he would never walk again. I had to control myself.

'Don't you dare even try to speak to me until I am calm enough to speak to you. Don't you dare!'

I could see him sink low into the bed as I spoke, shrinking under the power and anger in my voice. I turned and left the room, and as I walked past the nurses' station, they smiled at me.

One of them said, 'Well done. Be strong my dear.'

And I guessed she knew the rough road that was ahead of me.

As I stood to wait for an elevator, I had the urge to scream and cry and kick and throw a tantrum. Why was it just not possible for me to have a happy and peaceful life?

Did every man I know have to betray me, and what was I left with now?

No one.

The elevator doors opened, and I felt a surge of panic in case Evelyn was in it and then relief when she wasn't.

'You have God,' a voice in my head said to me all the way to my car.

It took me nearly two hours to get home in the treacherous rain and wind, but instead of going home I went to Minister Lyle's house. His wife Vera answered the door and gasped when she saw me, ushering me into the house immediately.

My sneakers squelched with every step, oozing little bubbles of water and my jacket dripped water onto the carpet, leaving a trail behind me as Vera maneuvered me into a bathroom and told me to wait there. A few minutes later she returned with a change of clothes.

'Put these on,' she ordered, and I meekly obeyed.

We sat in the living room and as I told them of what had transpired the past eight hours they were horrified and stunned. Once I had relived the sordid story, the realization that my life was in ruins hit me, and I felt wrought with sadness. I cried and cried. I wrung out the pain and hurt into huge chunks of tears and wails of despair.

'How could they do this?' I asked over and over again.

I hugged a cushion to my chest to prevent my heart from exploding. Vera comforted me as best she could. There wasn't much else she could do. Minister Lyle sat in silence contemplating all that he had heard, without a doubt silently praying.

Vera brought me a bowl of soup, insisting that I finish it all, and while I sipped at the soup slowly, we continued to discuss my predicament.

'How could Christians do this? Especially Evelyn, I mean, it was through her that I am a Christian today?'

I searched them for an answer.

'No Christian is safe from evil. In fact, it is the Christians that Satan wants most. Look at Peter he denied Christ; everyone has to be on guard from Satan every second of every day.'

'I can't understand it. Spencer kept on about this five-year plan; I still told you about it,' I pointed toward Minister Lyle in acknowledgment. 'He was adamant there were to be no babies until then and how could he act like there was nothing wrong and in the meantime, he is having an affair with my best friend? And all the time I thought it was Sian's baby. No wonder she did not want to tell him about it. Oh, I have been such a fool!'

I ranted on and on until my heart shattered and burst into a flood of grief.

'Stay here for the night. Let's pray together,' Minister Lyle said, and we held hands and prayed.

Chapter Thirty

I woke up in strange surroundings confused as to where I was, my head felt like a foggy cloud, and even the clothes I was wearing were strange. When I sat up and looked around the room, slowly the events of the previous day flooded back to the surface and rather than face reality, I allowed the pillow to caress my head while my heart pinned my body to the mattress; it was so heavy. The blankets smothered me in their covers of pity and shame while I wallowed in self-pity, sobbing my heart out.

The sun was trying to break through the dark clouds, and I wondered what the time was, and with deliberate movements, my body escaped the hold of the warm, soothing bed. I opened the bedroom door and peeked my head out, listening for any sound of life in the house.

Barefoot, I made my way to the living room and found no one. I looked around at this cozy home filled with photos of loved ones and modest furniture, and all I could feel was love; this is what a home should feel like, and it did not take a five-year plan to achieve it.

'Good morning,' a friendly voice thankfully interrupted my downcast thoughts.

'Good morning Vera, what time is it?'

'Eight-thirty, you had a good sleep I hope?'

'It seems I must have. I never sleep so late. Vera, thank you. I don't know what I would've done last night if you hadn't been so kind.'

I reached out to her and hugged her, I wanted to cling to her, but she gently pulled away.

'That's what friends are for - now how about I make some coffee, and you jump into a nice warm shower? I have more clothes you can borrow.'

'Yes, Mother,' I said and forced a smile onto my hideously drawn face.

The warm water ran over my exhausted body, and I tried to wash away the horrible images and thoughts of the hospital room.

I prayed softly, 'Oh Lord, please forgive me. Please forgive me for not putting you first in my life. For allowing the influence of others to control my commitment to you. I want to understand what you want me to do. Please guide me, Lord. In Jesus' name, Amen.'

I leaned forward against the wall resting my head on my arms; there was no way to tell the tears from the water.

When I got back to the guest bedroom, Vera had neatly laid out a skirt, tee-shirt and a navy blue jersey on the now made up bed. As I dressed, I looked around the room, the pale yellow walls, the avocado green checked curtains and light brown furniture helped to relax your mind. It was warm and soft and said, "Don't worry."

If only the walls could absorb my pain.

Vera welcomed me in the kitchen with warm coffee and toast with strawberry jam.

'I hope I haven't kept you away from anything important this morning?' I asked.

'Nope. You picked an easy day,' she smiled, 'do you want me to go with you to your apartment?'

'What am I going to do? I don't have parents to go to, and even if they were still alive, they would be of no help to me at all. I don't have any friends anymore and, well, we won't even talk about my so-called best friend! How could they?'

I felt the anger rising as my skin began to tingle, the hairs on my arms stood to attention as I felt the anxiety of my uncertain future and my failed past taking over my rational senses.

Vera quickly gathered where my thoughts were taking me, and she came to the rescue.

'So we will go to your apartment and then get whatever you need for the next few days because you are going to stay here. Lyle and I discussed it last night actually, and you have no say in the matter.'

She smiled reassuringly, and I wanted to cringe in shame that I was reduced to being dependent on someone else for survival.

'Thank you,' I said not knowing what else to say.

I stared dolefully at the countertop while Vera talked about nothing important.

'Evelyn was the one that helped me through the Boyd episode, and now she does this. I just can't understand it. It seems I am destined to be hurt and left alone by everyone that is supposed to love me and that I love, which is worse!' I spoke aloud trying to sort out the confused rambling in my brain.

Vera stood up and took the dishes to the sink. Her kitchen was light, the cupboards were in need of replacement, but she overcame that with bright red curtains and ornaments. Your eyes focused on the red before you noticed the old cupboards. The kitchen had the feel of comfort, happily lived in comfort.

'You are not alone. You have Lyle and me, and God will never leave you. I know you are confused – we all are – but don't give up on God's plan for you. Please don't.'

She came back to where I was sitting and held my hands, her eyes pleading with me.

'God loves you; He will get you through this.'

She gently pulled me to my feet.

'Right, let's go to your place and get it over with.'

We drove in silence to my apartment, and on the way we passed my parents' old property – a new house stood where the burnt remains had been.

'Hope those people have a better future there,' I said sadly.

We entered my apartment; my heart was pounding wildly, constricting my breathing and my nerves. I threw the keys in the bowl as I had always done and looked about the dwelling. It was bland and had no feeling of the love and welcome I felt in Vera's house. The only sign that two people who had supposedly loved each other lived there was the large framed photo of us on our wedding day. I walked up to it and took it off the wall, and for a few seconds I stared at it, and then I threw it on the floor, shattering the glass into a mass of small pieces, now it felt just as my heart did. Vera simply locked at me without judging or condoning me.

I packed a bag of clothes and toiletries, and while in the study packing up my work-related things, I phoned Rodger. He was stunned. He battled to find any words to say, except to tell me to take two days off.

As I walked out of the study, there was fidgeting at the front door, and it slowly opened from the outside. I took loud gasps of air to help get the influx of oxygen into my lungs. I felt the panic exploding within me as I stared at Spencer standing in the doorway. Vera excused herself and forced her way passed him to stand in the passageway outside.

'Kaye,' Spencer said hesitantly, walking toward me.

'Stay where you are. Do not come near me!'

I spat the words at him, surprised that I was even able to speak. I felt a flush of heat move to my cheeks inflaming them.

'Please Kaye, I can explain, I didn't mean it to happen, it just happened…I'm so sorry Kaye, I…'

Before he was able to continue his pathetic excuse for an explanation I picked up a coffee cup that was standing on the side table next to the couch and threw it at him. He was too late to avoid the flying object, and it connected with the side of his head before breaking into a few large pieces.

'HOW COULD YOU?' I screamed.

My brain somehow remembered to pick up my bags before I pushed him aside as I dashed for the door. He staggered still dazed from the bump the coffee cup had given him, and he was too slow to try and stop me.

Vera took a bag from me and held my arm as we ran to the lift, the doors shut and not a second later Spencer was trying to stop me from leaving, calling me from the other side of the closing doors.

We ran to the car, and as soon as I was around the bend and out of sight, I pulled the car over to the shoulder of the road. My body convulsed with the spasms of my broken heart. I tried to control my shaking legs and continue driving, but it was impossible. Vera held me firmly, calming my tightly wound up nerves with prayer. When I broke away from her finally, she got out and walked around to the driver's side while I slid over into the passenger seat. She drove back to her house cautiously – not having driven my car before – and also avoided driving passed my parents' house.

While I unpacked my few belongings, I visualized Spencer's head connecting with the coffee cup. Since when did I have such a temper? I was shocked at my behavior. Who was this person I had become?

'Vera, I am sorry you had to witness that. I am so shocked at the way I reacted.'

'Don't be sorry. Don't ever be sorry. We never know how we will react in a situation until we are in it. But I must say, I have never seen a coffee cup fly so sweetly,' she said with her lips turned up at the corners, on the verge of laughter.

I giggled, and before long Vera was dramatizing, with the aid of her hands, the event for Minister Lyle. She picked up a coffee cup and visually showed him (without actually letting the cup go) how it had flown across the room and demonstrated against his head where it had landed on Spencer's. I watched her, amused by her storytelling, but I was reliving it with Spencer's face in front of me, and it made me want to shrivel up in a hollow grave and disappear.

Minister Lyle calmly took the cup from Vera and placed it back down on the kitchen counter. 'Don't you get any ideas from Kaye,' he smiled.

He was not too sure if he should laugh or scold me for my behavior.

Living with Lyle and Vera for the next few days was what I needed to reflect, rethink and re-evaluate my life. Had I not been with them I hate to think of how bitter I would have become and how far I might have strayed from God's righteous path. I shuddered at the thought.

Chapter Thirty-One

I felt everyone's eyes upon me as I walked into the office and passed all the cubicles until I finally reached mine at the end of the room. It had been a week since Spencer's accident and the betrayal, and by now they all knew about it. The whole town, as with any gossip, knew about it, and I was surprised it was not the headline news.

Hidden away in my cubicle I felt safe, Rodger was like a security guard or a Rottweiler protecting my little area of space. It was when he was out of the office that I became aware of the curious eyes watching me.

The first few times my phone rang I gave a tiny jump and nervously answered it expecting it to be either Spencer or Evelyn, but by the time the afternoon came along I was plunged back into my work, submerged in my world of journalism and feeling a lot more relaxed. When the phone rang, I answered without reservation.

'Don't hang up,' his voice pleaded.

I hung up instantly, flustered and annoyed that he had disrupted my concentration and the comfortable space I had occupied. Now I was back in that realm of being nervous and insecure. Before I allowed the anxiety to take over, I remembered what Minister Lyle had said to me before leaving for work that morning.

'If you feel you are losing control, go to a place where you can be alone and pray, pray and pray some more until you find peace come over you. Then go back and handle the situation with God in control.'

I went to the bathroom. After several minutes of desperate prayer, I heard someone enter the room.

'Kaye, you still in here?' Kiki called out.

'Be out in a minute,' I answered still sitting on the closed toilet.

'I'll wait for you at your desk,' she replied as she left the bathroom.

When I got back to my desk, Kiki was reading from a single sheet of paper while leaning against the screen divider. She was, as always, dressed in jeans, a buttoned shirt, and hiking boots, always on the ready to take off for a story. Her blonde hair was tied back loosely so that there was more falling out than actually in the ponytail.

'Everything okay?' she questioned me.

'Yep. He called, and I hung up.'

'Let's go out for coffee.'

She indicated with her eyes in a rolling motion that all the staff would be listening. I understood that she either had something confidential to tell me or she was simply sympathetic. Either way, I was happy to leave with her. The twenty-odd pairs of eyes followed us all the way to the doors until we exited the office.

'So I don't want to know all your personal stuff, I'm not a gossip monger as you well know, but Rodger did tell me what happened. I'm sorry Kaye,' she said once we sat, settled and the waitress had taken our order and left us alone.

We sat in a corner nook of the restaurant. The orange circle patterns on the walls made me dizzy.

'Thanks, Kiki, I'm still trying to believe it, let alone understand it.'

'I know it's early days still but do you have any idea what you are going to do? I have a reason for asking.'

'Nope – not even given any thought to anything.'

The sadness groaned through my voice.

'Okay so I got a telex this morning,' she said pulling out the page she had been reading at my desk, 'the sister company in the Cape Town office is looking for a journalist. I have a friend that is dying to get me there, so she keeps sending me the positions whenever they become available.'

She handed me the page.

'If you want the position I will tell her to keep it for you.'

I read it, waited until the waitress had put down our order of coffee and milk tart on the table and left before replying.

'You don't want the position?'

'My husband cannot leave his job here, so what would be the point?'

'This sounds too good to be true. It might be what I need right now!'

'That's what I thought. The people at the Cape office are awesome; I'm sure you will fit in well with them.'

'How long before they need an answer?'

'I'll ask her to hold it for a week for you. After that, they will advertise it.'

While I picked at my milk tart, Kiki told me more about the Cape Town office; based in Strand about eighty kilometers from the center of Cape Town, and it was a coastal town so I would still be near the ocean.

'Rodger won't be happy if I go.'

'He will understand. You need a fresh start and new scenery, and there is no place more beautiful than the Cape to help you do that,' Kiki said with such confidence that I had to believe her.

Before we left the restaurant, she handed me another piece of paper from her notebook. I read the name and phone number.

'What is this?'

'Divorce lawyer. He is brilliant, and he's also my brother.'

She grinned as she answered.

In Vera's kitchen, I showed her both pages and waited for her response as if I needed her to tell me what to do.

'So did he phone you again after you hung up?' she asked first, before discussing the papers and the messages on them.

'No. I think he can still feel the bump from the coffee cup,' I chuckled at the memory of the incident.

'What does your heart tell you to do?'

'You mean besides beating them both senseless?'

'Kaye, I know you're bitter right now, but you must not make decisions with a hard heart. How long before you have to give them an answer for this job?'

'A week, and yes I know you're right, but when I think about it, I can't explain what goes through me. When he phoned, I had to do what Lyle suggested and go to the bathroom and pray like crazy.'

'It's going to be a long road ahead with many, many bumps but Kiki is probably right in suggesting a change of scenery.'

When Minister Lyle came home, we sat in their cozy living room and discussed all the pros and cons of the position in

Cape Town. There were more pros than cons. He did, however, suggest that he sit with Spencer and me to discuss our situation. After I had done a lot of protesting, I was finally convinced that it had to happen. I only agreed on the condition that Vera was allowed to sit in with me, and if I was unable to maintain my self-control, at any time, that I could leave.

When Minister Lyle phoned me later the next day to confirm the meeting with Spencer for that evening, my body crumbled with anxiety. Kiki was at her desk sorting through photos, so I joined her for the last two hours of the working day, rather than wallow on my own.

How was I supposed to get through this meeting?

Before leaving with Vera to Lyle's office at the church building he phoned to inform me that Evelyn had requested to be at the meeting. I growled at him for consenting to it and almost pulled out altogether. Vera dragged me back to the living room amid my ranting and sat me down on their worn couch.

'Let's pray,' she said calmly and took my hands.

On the way to the building, she gave me a little pink pill to chew.

'It will calm you down a little,' she offered, and I took it gratefully.

I chewed and chewed viciously, hoping that whatever chemical it emitted would get to work on my erratic nerves immediately.

Spencer and Evelyn were already in Minister Lyle's office when we arrived. I'd hope to be there first. My legs were jelly, and although Vera held tightly onto me, they wobbled with each step. She opened the door to his office, gripping my arm, guiding me toward the chair that was vacant and ready for me to sit in, thankfully on the opposite side of the room to where Spencer and Evelyn sat.

Minister Lyle's office was not very large, so even if I was on the opposite side, I was still too close for comfort. It was like his home, just the basics, nothing fancy, with a touch of love beaming from the photos of himself and Vera that hung on the wall behind him.

Minister Lyle stood up, and Spencer immediately did so too. Evelyn remained seated with her eyes focused on her swollen belly. I sat as quickly as possible knowing my legs were about to give in at any second. I shoved my hands under my legs to stop them from shaking and planted my feet apartment on the carpeted floor; the slightest movement caused them to vibrate like a jackhammer.

My heart pulsated in my ears so loudly that it was difficult to hear Lyle speak. I searched for something I was able to focus on other than the pathetic expressions of my enemies.

Minister Lyle opened the meeting with a prayer, and I tried with all my might to focus on what he was saying in his prayer, to focus on God, to allow God to control me and not try and control myself. The latter, if allowed, would result in bloodshed.

I sat in silence, glued to my seat, hearing the faint sniffs from Evelyn, daring not to speak while Minister Lyle spoke for all of us concerned. Vera sat next to me her arm spread across my shoulders in support.

'Spencer, will you speak first please?' Minister Lyle asked.

My husband looked at me with those blue eyes, and I wondered how much truth had ever been in them. He tried several times to speak, and each time his voice was overcome by the lump of guilt shoved tight in his throat.

After several attempts and with tears streaming out of his blue eyes he said, 'I am so sorry Kaye, please forgive me.'

He bent his head and held it in his hands while his shoulders shook with remorse. Evelyn lifted her hand and rested it on his back, rubbing it compassionately which infuriated me. Did she have to show me how affectionate she was toward my husband in front of me?

I moved my leg, and Vera instinctively knew I was about to run or attack them, either action was highly possible, so she tightened her arm around my shoulder.

'Let God control you,' she whispered in my ear.

I gripped the chair with my hands tucked in again under my legs, fighting to find any words to say.

'Oh please forgive us,' Evelyn choked out softly as she still stared at her lap, but still with her one hand caressing Spencer's back.

I shivered with anger; I shivered with disappointment, I shivered from pain and a broken heart. I shivered, fighting the hatred swirling within me. I took deep breaths for several minutes, the silence, other than my deep breaths and sniffing from Spencer and Evelyn, was thick and threatening.

'How long?'

They all looked at me and feared the hard, sad and bitter expression reaching over my face. 'How long has this been going on? It's clearly a few months since she,' which was spat out like venom, 'is a few months pregnant.'

There was silence.

'How long?' I demanded.

Spencer lifted his head although his eyes did not connect with mine.

'Eight months. When you went to do that interview in Pretoria and Sian broke up with Evelyn; we never meant for it to happen, Kaye, I'm so sorry.'

'Eight months?' I shrieked. 'Eight months? We have only been married for eighteen months, and in all that time you never thought to stop?'

They hung their heads in shame. However, it did not soften my resolve or my words.

'You dare to ask me to forgive you now? You are both nothing but the Devil's agents! Despicable, heartless, loathsome liars and cheats.'

I took a breath and swallowed the lump jamming my throat as water flowed down my cheeks but before I could continue to throw my abuse at them the despair in my soul drenched me, and I burst into blubbering sobs, unable to say anymore.

I indicated to Minister Lyle that I was leaving, and Vera helped me stand up, supporting me as I had to force my reluctant body to move. I felt sorry for Vera having to deal with my ranting hysteria all the way home. My heart felt as if it would stop beating at any given second it was so crushed.

Chapter Thirty-Two

The new generation swamped Baggies Beach. It amused me to watch them and relive my special happy times spent there, as in a few hours I would be leaving this sanctuary of my soul. I would have to find a new place where to grab at peace and tranquillity.

I lay on my towel-clad only in my green bikini with the sun baking my flesh, my old surfboard occupying the sand next to me. I needed to absorb the last sunrays of the day, and this would probably be the last time I would catch them here on Baggies Beach. Once I left on the train to Cape Town, there was nothing here left for me.

Forcing myself to get up off the towel, put on my white shorts and a pale yellow top. I picked up my board and bag and went to the café, ordered a cheese and tomato sandwich and while that was being made I shoved my board onto the roof racks of my car, securing it tightly.

I sat at one the tables on the paved area outside the café and while eating my sandwich it slowly dawned on me that this was the last time I would watch these waves, see the sun set in this magical paradise and the last time that I would eat this disgusting food. I giggled at myself.

'Hi, Kaye.'

'Rosalie hello, how are you?'

She sat down next to me.

'We always seem to bump into each other here,' she said with a pleasant smile.

'Not for long.'

The bitter tone deflected from my tongue.

'Kaye, I am so sorry, I'm sure you're aware that everyone knows what happened.'

'Let's see to which incident you are referring to – Boyd, my parents or Spencer? It seems I have a lot to offer the world regarding drama.'

'All of them I guess. You did not deserve any of it, Kaye.'

She wanted to say more but shut herself up instead.

'Thanks, Rosalie, sorry I don't mean to be so sarcastic.'

We both just stared at the ocean for a few minutes before she spoke again, 'Seems like forever since we used to be them.'

She nudged her chin toward the young school kids playing touch rugby on the sand.

'Pity time doesn't stand still.'

I felt my heart stutter as the vivid image of our school days and friends bounced through the memory cupboard door that kept swinging open – Boyd and York in the forefront. It hurt. It hurt so much.

'I'm going to Cape Town tomorrow morning. I had to spend my last few hours here,' I said wiping away the single tear that escaped.

'It is probably the best thing for you, a fresh start and all that.'

'So they say.'

'Will you stay in touch with me, please?'

She took out a pen and paper from her bag and wrote her number down then handed it to me. I was touched as even though we had never really been friends, only simply part of the crowd, Rosalie had always been exceptionally kind and friendly toward me.

'Yes, I will, thank you, Rosalie.'

I meant it too.

We both left the beach at the same time, and after she had given me a sincere, affectionate hug goodbye, I took one last look at the ocean, said goodbye to it and drove away for the last time.

I made a detour to Vera, and Minister Lyle's house passed my parents' old property. I parked my car on the sidewalk opposite the driveway and looked at the now grand house that occupied the ground.

'Well Daddy and Mommy, wherever you are now, thanks for nothing,' I finally said, started the engine of my Beetle and drove away.

It was early in the morning; the sun was not even up yet. Minister Lyle, Vera and I watched as my car was loaded onto the cargo train for its journey to Cape Town. My train was arriving in three hours' time.

Durban Central Station was abuzz with loud sounds of trains coming to a standstill as the journey ended there. Feet bustled along, and announcements constantly made over the PA system. Rodger and Kiki joined Minister Lyle, Vera and me in the small restaurant at the station, their steak and kidney pies were scrumptious but perhaps not at five in the morning. I felt genuinely touched that Rodger and Kiki had made the effort to see me off, and I hoped that we would stay in contact and perhaps even see one another again in the future.

The thought of what my future held terrified me. A strange town, with strange people and a strange new job, scared the daylights out of me and yet there was a determination about me to hit it head on and move on with my life. I had done it before; I could do it again. I had to do it again.

Waving one last time out of the window of my compartment, I eased back in and slid the window down, shutting that chapter of my life forever. I picked up the envelope Rodger had shoved into my hand as he'd hugged me goodbye. Five hundred Rand and a farewell card signed by his wife and him left me with an urge to jump from the train and run back to the life and people that had not let me down. I took out the pieces of paper from my pocket that had contact people and phone numbers that Minister Lyle and Kiki had given me and placed them inside the envelope from Rodger.

Exhausted from lack of sleep and crowded thoughts I pulled the bed out and climbed on it. The chug-chug and rocking motion drew the sleep I desired upon me very quickly.

Two days later I got off the train at Cape Town Central Station, lugging my bags and my surfboard onto the trolley I had nabbed that had been standing close to my carriage. I had no idea what Kiki's friend Lilith looked like, or as she preferred to be called Li. Brown hair and brown eyes Kiki had said – well that certainly narrowed it down.

Deciding that I should start walking and hopefully I would bump into her. I gave a big heave, and slowly the overloaded trolley moved forward. I felt grimy and dirty hoping that I did not smell too bad as well. The jeans and a green long-sleeved cotton shirt with a black sweater and white sneakers, at least, were clean and fresh. I could not say the same for the garments from the first leg of the trip, though!

As I pushed the trolley, which was probably heavier than my luggage, a short brunette lady with brown eyes and a wide smile greeted me.

'Are you Kaye?'

'Yes, you must be Li.'

'At last, I was so afraid I would miss you, and you would land up in Khayelitsha.'

'Where?'

She laughed at my ignorance and helped me push the trolley to her car. She was as lively and bubbly as Kiki had said she would be. She had a Kombi for obvious reasons; she had a handful of children; their remnants were all over the car.

From Cape Town Central to Gordon's Bay Li gave me a running commentary as we drove; it was such a beautiful part of the country; I had never imagined the mountains to be so beautiful.

Li had four gorgeous, mischievous, yet well-mannered boys. Their eyes sparkled at the sight of new prey when I walked into her house. The boys were between the ages of three and seven and when I asked her if she'd had them on purpose she laughed and replied that she had. I wondered how someone could be so brave.

I settled in the guest room without unpacking my case – I would only be in it for one night – then I made my way back to the kitchen. Li had taken the day off which was the reason the boys were also at home; they were usually in a daycare, the eldest in grade one while their parents were at work.

'When we've finished eating we can go to the apartment so you can make sure it is as you expected; then we can make a turn by the office. Gerome is eager to meet you. In the morning, your car should have arrived then we can go and fetch it.'

'Thank you for all your help. I really, really appreciate it. Is he a good boss?'

'He is demanding and often a bit unfair if you get on the wrong side of him, but stay out of his way, do your work, and you will be fine.'

'Shoo, I am so nervous now.'

'You will be fine. Kiki told me why you moved here, hope that's okay. I can't imagine going through what you've gone through.'

'Then don't imagine it because it's awful,' I replied perhaps a bit too harshly, but the words slipped out without any thought.

'Well new scenery, new life,' she smiled.

I felt a pang of guilt at being so sarcastic.

The one bedroom apartment was perfect for me, for now. It was in a small complex, there were only six apartments in the building, and it was not too far from the sea. Gordon's Bay was simply perfect. It was very much like Warner Beach, a small community and still a village, not a commercial town. I looked forward to moving in on the weekend.

Gingerly I walked behind Li as we entered the office. It had a similar set up as my old office, so I felt a little more relaxed. Gerome was sitting in his huge office chair behind his overflowing desk. He was a large man, the "all business" type and had a sweating problem – his shirt was half wet, and his forehead dotted with drops of perspiration. I shuddered in disgust and hoped he never stood too close to me.

He greeted me in a deep, gruff voice becoming of his size.

'Welcome, Kaye. Li will show you to your desk and tomorrow we will go over all the necessary,' he said and directed his attention back to his desk.

Li gave me a tour of the office and showed me where I would be working; I was not moved to be excited or eager to start, I simply felt numb.

Once I was in my little Beetle driving behind Li so as not to get lost, I slowly started feeling more at ease, as if a part of my hometown was still with me.

Chapter Thirty-Three

It was strange to see the sun setting over the ocean as opposed to in Natal. The Atlantic Ocean was so much colder, and I did not venture into the water further than my feet. The sunset was breath-taking, setting off the mountains surrounding this little town in a hue of blues and greys. I was simply awestruck and immediately fell in love with this little paradise on earth, and I prayed silently that the people were as lovely.

With Vera's excellent directions I found my way to the church in Strand and instantly knew I wanted to worship there. The building was quaint, grabbing you in a welcoming embrace as you entered. My nervousness got thwarted as people, young and old, introduced themselves to me, offering love and friendship almost instantly. Most of the young adults my age were away on a fellowship weekend, so I would only meet them at Bible study on Wednesday evening. If they were anything like the people I had just met, then I was going to be just fine. I could feel it in my bones.

Sleep eluded me the first few nights in my new apartment. I felt lonely, so very lonely.

Why had these things happened to me?

What was the lesson I had to learn?

Where did God want me to end up?

Would I ever find happiness?

Happiness that wasn't only short term, but happiness that would last forever?

What did God want of me?

I prayed endlessly, prayed for answers to my never-ending questions. I just wanted to understand why I could not have happiness. I begged God to help me understand. I wished I were able to change the past, knowing it was impossible.

My heart was wrenched away from the world as I painfully relived my past, Boyd shot into my vision, the smile that softened his harsh features, and next to him was York. York, the one I thought would never leave me or disappoint me. Pain ripped through my heart and into my eyes and throat. I gulped and exploded inside, distraught with the lot I was dealt. The burnt remains of my parents floated past York's face, and I screamed into my pillow. Spencer and Evelyn held a baby, looking happy and content as their small family drifted to the forefront of my mind, erasing my zombie parents. I screamed again and shot up into a sitting position on my bed, my skin cold and clammy, my eyes wide with fear and my heart pounding like bullets against my chest.

I staggered to the kitchen for a glass of water to drown the crazy dreams. Thanks be to a pink pill Vera had given me that I still had in my bag; I eventually managed to get about three hours of undisturbed sleep.

Li had given me very detailed directions on how to get to the office from my apartment, and yet my muddled and tired mind and body still managed to get me lost. Fretting, I pulled my car in at a petrol station and asked for directions, and the attendant showed me the building just twenty meters away from where I was standing. How had I missed it?

My arms were full of my typewriter, files, handbag and other personal items, so I walked cautiously to my desk – all I needed was to trip and make an idiot of myself before I even sat down for the first time. I noticed most the other employees had photos of loved ones all over their screened walls. What photos might I possibly put on my walls?

All eyes were watching me as I put my things on my desk with a thump, if it was too loud, well then that was just too bad. The urge to bolt and run forever was brimming and wanted to boil over at any second.

I was glad I had worn my long green cotton skirt and a white top with my wedge sandals as I noticed most of the ladies were all rather well dressed.

With my few belongings packed away I was ready to start working, but since Gerome had not arrived yet I had nothing to do, so I sat at my desk staring at the blank screened walls.

'Hi there, I see you've settled in,' Li finally arrived with a warm, friendly smile.

'Yes thank you, I don't know what to do yet, though.'

'Gerome has just arrived so let's see him shall we?'

Over the next few weeks, I was given a few small assignments to do, and I handled them well enough considering I got lost each and every time, and every time I wanted to burst into sorrowful tears, as it reminded me of exactly how alone I was in an unfamiliar town among strangers.

It was our weekly meeting, and as usual, I sat in the back of the room, present but absent at the same time. After Gerome had said his bit and when everyone was leaving the boardroom, he asked me to remain behind.

He did not give me time to start stressing about what I had or had not done since he spoke immediately 'You settled in okay?' he asked.

'Yes, fine, thank you.'

'Let's go to my office,' he said and indicated the way with his hand.

I knew I was in trouble, and my heart sank.

'Sit,' he said, offering me a chair opposite his desk.

I sat.

'So your articles have been fine, but I must say they are not as passionate as I was led to believe they would be. I don't think you have the passion anymore to be the journalist I was told you were.'

He stared at me expectantly, waiting for my reply.

'I am sorry, I guess I am in a bit of a slump still. I will fix it, I promise.'

Did I want to fix it or did I want to run away?

It was a toss-up.

'Well, I want to offer you a solution. How would you like to learn the ropes in the layout and design section? I know you have your degree in journalism and all that, but I figured you wouldn't get lost in the streets anymore,' he paused with a teasing smirk on his face, 'and you might find it interesting.'

I didn't hesitate in my decision.

'Yes, I'd like that. Thank you for being so kind to me,' I replied expressionlessly.

'Well, let's just say I know how you're feeling right now.'

He did not offer any further explanation but instead told me who to go and see in the office on the floor below.

The move to the new department took me one day, and after a week, I was already changing my attitude and smiling a lot more in a single day than I had in months.

The group of young adults at church were so enthusiastic, vibrant and were such a bunch of diverse characters. I was welcomed into the fold with sympathy at first, but it was soon forgotten and replaced with affection and encouragement. They were forever planning some or other activity, which was great for me as the weekends were mostly occupied in their company rather than alone in my apartment.

When I spoke to Vera and Rosalie during our weekly phone calls, they both noticed each week how much better I sounded every time we spoke. I did feel better and far more positive, but somehow that nagging bitterness edged over my tendrils just as a reminder. I had to allow God to cure me completely, but it was just so difficult to let go.

I walked into Bible study on a freezing cold evening, I had not known cold like this in my life and had someone warned me how cold the Cape was I still would not have expected this. I had on a thick jacket I'd purchased that morning, sweatpants, a thick jersey and the thickest boots I had ever seen in my life. Everyone seems to find my adversity to the weather rather amusing.

I made myself comfortable on a couch alongside a few of the ladies and readily got to know them a little more. I heard laughter coming from outside that pricked my ears. Switching off from the conversation I strained even harder to try and hear that sound once more.

There it was again; I had undeniably heard it.

'Excuse me,' I said hurriedly, and abruptly got off the couch and made my way outside the room into the courtyard, instantly feeling the chill nip in my bones.

The men were playing the fool as usual and also entertaining the younger boys. I heard it again and looked toward the sound I was so interested in, my ears now pricked to attention. I took a few paces closer to the laughter. The men had gathered in a huddle wrestling for a ball – go figure – and I stood on the brim of their pile up, and as they loosened the hold they had on each other; they unfolded like a napkin. I gasped. It couldn't be!

'York!' I squealed.

Everyone went silent, glancing between York and me, as confused as we probably were.

He was still half lying and half sitting on the ground, and I watched as his face went from that of a naughty boy to an expression of disbelief as he registered who I was within seconds. He stood up not taking his eyes from me, his mouth open, and his bottom lip fell to the ground until he finally responded.

'Kaye!' he cried and in one leap he had his arms wrapped around me, swinging me from side to side, his laughter rampant.

He moved back away from me still holding his hands on my shoulders, gluing his eyes to mine. 'What, what are you doing here chicky?'

His smile covered his face. We were by now the center of attention as everyone had come out of the "chilling room" and was watching our reunion.

'I...I...live here,' I stammered.

'What? Since when?'

While I stared at his bright glowing face, the pain of his disappearance clouded my mind.

'You left without any contact. Why?'

My face grew downcast, dragging his with it. Before he was able to answer, we were asked to go inside to begin the study. York gently put his arm around my shoulders and walked with me, but as we were about to enter the doorway, he stopped.

'Where's Spencer?' he questioned me, looking about him nervously.

'Not here,' I replied grimacing.

He smiled again putting his arm around me until we were in our seats, and then he sat closely next to me throughout the study. It was so difficult for me to concentrate as I was so confused, with so many questions I needed to ask him; and there was also the continuous flow of eyes watching us, everyone was in an above normal state of curious.

Chapter Thirty-Four

York was acting like an excited boy reaching for his first football, eager to go and play with it. I was ranging between anger and complete happiness.

He looked so well, his hair was a lot shorter, and it suited him better than I had ever imagined it would. He wore the same glasses that graced his more mature features. Mature features, yet he still carried the boyish childlike face I remembered.

I was delighted to see him still wearing the necklace I had given him, and my hands automatically held the silver cross dangling from my neck under my thick jersey.

I followed York after study to a restaurant on the beachfront in Strand leaving everyone wondering about our connection to each other.

After ordering coffee and an apple pie I blurted out, 'You left just like Boyd did. Why?'

He put his hands over mine that were fiddling with the napkin.

'Before I answer your question, and I will, I promise, first tell me where Spencer is.'

I told him my pathetic story; anger and disappointment fell off every spoken word, and the response in his expression went from shock to horror to anger. His face went red as I spoke, his lips pulled back tightly as if biting back what he wanted to say.

When I had finished with my tale of woe and had brought him up to date on my move to the Cape and the divorce two weeks ago, I looked up from the tablecloth I had been studying intently only to see tears dripping from behind York's glasses. His face was ashen. He took his glasses off and wiped his eyes with the sleeve of his grey sweater, then put them back on before speaking in a croaky voice

'Kaye, I'm so sorry. How could I have left you when I was supposed to be your friend? If I ever see that man again…'

He scrunched his lips together seething at the thought of what he might do. He shifted in his seat, picked off a piece of the apple pie that had arrived during my story, put it in his mouth and then continued speaking.

'After you came back from your honeymoon, Spencer phoned me. Before I could even ask how you were doing he told me never to contact you again; you were his wife now, and he would take care of you. He said our friendship was way too close for his liking, and it was best for me to break away from you.'

He stopped talking probably in fright at the horrified look on my face when the blood drained from it.

'He did what?' I asked incredulously, not believing what I had just heard. 'We were friends before he came along, you didn't have to listen to him!'

'He was your husband; he had every right to.'

'No, he didn't.'

'Kaye, what did you expect me to do, phone you and tell you your husband was a jerk? Would you have believed me and if you had confronted him he would've made me out to be a troublemaker and then I would have been told to leave you alone in any case? I thought it best to do as he said, for your sake. But Kaye what he did to you…I…I, flip it, I want to hurt him. And Evelyn, really?'

He tried to make constructive sentences to voice his opinion while his hands tore the paper napkin into shreds. I smiled hoping to lighten his mood even if I was hurting from the stabs of regret and pain.

'So what about you? Married? Engaged? Girlfriend?' I shrugged my shoulders in question.

'No, no, not me. I had a girlfriend in Jo'burg, but when this offer came up for a partnership here, she did not want to move, so I left her there. It wasn't that serious besides.'

'York, I'm so happy to find you again, who would've thought I would find you here?'

He smiled back at me and held my free hand as we finished our apple pie.

'Have you ever heard from Boyd again?' I asked quietly.

He fidgeted uncomfortably for a few seconds with his fork.

'So you have not heard? I was wondering if you had but was too afraid to ask.'

'Heard what? Tell me.'

He took a deep breath and slowly let it out.

'He died Kaye.'

Before he continued, he made sure I was okay with this newsflash.

'What?' The word filtered out of my mouth as my lips quivered.

I struggled to say, 'What happened?'

York patted my hand and wiped away the tears that floated down my face.

'He was shot a few months ago. That's all I know.'

'His parents…How did they take it?'

He shook his head, 'His mother had to be hospitalized.'

With my elbows on the table, I rested my head in my hands and allowed myself to cry softly. York called the waiter, paid our bill and gently lifted me at my elbow and guided me toward the exit door, across the road, and onto the beach.

We sat on the low wall facing the sea. The cold night cut the air and bit into my flesh viciously, freezing the liquid in my body and instantly my teeth began to chatter.

'It's too cold out here, are you okay to drive? I'll follow you home, and we can meet again tomorrow, how about that?'

I nodded.

As we walked back to our cars York kept me close to his side with his arm around me.

'I can't believe you still have this piece of junk,' he said as I opened the car door.

I turned around and threw my arms around him holding him so close to me, still in awe that I was able to.

'Don't be mean to my baby,' I giggled as I released him.

When we arrived at my apartment York made sure I got in safely and then left. I soaked in a hot bath to warm my cold bones and relished the idea of York in my life again.

Was York really back in my life or was this all a dream?

I collapsed with laughter when I finally convinced myself it was true.

I phoned Rosalie first thing in the morning before I left for work. She was gobsmacked to hear that York was back in my life but immensely happy for me at the same time. Now I would not feel so alone and like a stranger.

I walked into the office with an extra bounce in my step; it was obvious to everyone, and if they asked what was up with me, I told them.

'I have my friend back. God is good.'

That's all they needed to know.

I had to wait for lunch time until York phoned me. While we spoke over the phone, a smile stuck to my face.

'Tonight have dinner with my parents...'

'They live here too?' I couldn't believe it.

'Yes, they retired and moved here too...Anyway, please have dinner with them, they will be so thrilled to see you. I won't tell them you're coming; they will be so surprised. They don't live too far from you actually.'

'Shame you're cruel, your poor mother might have a heart attack!' I laughed.

'She will be so happy to see you, please say yes,' he begged.

'Okay...' I still wanted to lay down a few conditions, but instead, he interrupted me.

'Good. I will pick you up at about six-thirty.'

I agreed and asked if I should bring anything with me to which he huffed at me.

'So one thing has been bothering me,' I said 'how come I have not seen you at study before last night? I have been attending for a while now, and you haven't been there?'

'My parents and I went on a road trip for three weeks, and before that, I was busy with a course in Pretoria, so I have been away for at least two months.'

'Aaah, suppose that explains it then.'

'Kaye,' he hesitated for a bit, 'it is so good to see you.'

'I still can't believe it's true. I keep waiting to wake up from the dream. I heard your laugh from the "chilling room" and was so afraid that my ears were deceiving me.'

'You heard my laugh?' He burst out laughing, that beautiful infectious laugh.

I laughed with him; it was impossible not to.

He fetched me at six-thirty and drove around the corner and up the road about fifty meters to his parents' house. They truly did live close to me.

'Kayeeeeeeee!' Aubrey, York's mother, screeched when York stepped aside, so they were able to see me.

She engulfed me in a massive hug.

'Oh my goodness it is so wonderful to see you!' York's father pried her away to get his turn to hug and welcome me.

'You are still so lovely Kaye, what a wonderful surprise!'

I was overwhelmed by their enthusiasm. I expected them to be surprised and jubilant at my appearance, but such a display of affection was far more than I'd imagined.

What a pleasant evening it was, once the initial morbid past was told, and all questions were exhausted, then true friendship and happiness filled the house. I grabbed it; I swallowed it, I drank it in, I relished it. It was fantastic.

Chapter Thirty-Five

York and I became increasingly joined at the hip, always together unless we were at work. It was truly fabulous to have my friend back. I was pleasantly surprised to find out that York's parents had committed their lives to God through the influence and encouragement of their son.

A beautiful bond was developing between Aubrey and me, and we met for lunch sometimes during the week, Li joined us on a few occasions, and we enjoyed the time we spent together on weekends too. After church almost every Sunday we would barbeque at York's parents' house.

Li's boisterous boys adored York, and naturally so. He had the energy and childlike attitude to entertain the boys for hours on end. They often got banned to the playroom, without much coercion from Li.

'He will be a great father one day,' Li mentioned while we packed dishes away in her chaotic kitchen.

'Yes, he will. I find it hard to believe no one has snatched him up yet.'

Li did not reply, but the corners of her mouth twitched as if she knew a secret and was not going to tell anyone.

Before setting the phone down on one of my many phone calls to Rosalie she excitely told me to watch the mailbox for a wedding invitation. I was so thrilled for her and Charl. They had dated while at school for a while, broken up and a year ago had fallen in love again at the infamous Showboat. The wedding would be in February.

As expected the invitation arrived, and as I fidgeted with the creamed color invite, I pondered whether it would be wise for me to return to Warner Beach so soon.

'What's wrong chicky?' York asked sensing my pensive mood.

I flipped over the invitation in my hand and passed it to him. He read it quickly, already in the know about the wedding.

'So, what's the problem?'

He looked at me, and I stood up from the couch and walked over to the kitchen, opened the fridge and refilled my glass with orange juice. He stood up and joined me in the kitchen refilling his glass as well.

With Aubrey's help, we had managed to make my apartment very cozy with warm colors and bright cushions.

'I don't know if I am ready to go back. What if I bump into Boyd's parents or even worse, Spencer and Evelyn? What if the memories are too much for me to handle?' I looked at him, begging him to smooth my worries.

'Well! The invitation does say Kaye and partner, so I will go along – thank you for the invitation!'

He had such a naughty smile creasing his cheeks.

'And if we fly on Saturday morning and fly back Sunday afternoon there will be little chance of bumping into anyone. We can stay at my aunt's house, she will love having her favorite nephew visit and if you like, Sunday morning early we can go to Baggies and then go to church before we come home.'

He finished his sentence and gulped down the rest of his juice, put his glass in the sink and turned his focus back to me, waiting for my response.

'Seems like you have it all planned out already. Are you sure you don't mind?'

'It will be fun, and once you've covered this hurdle, you will feel far more confident, trust me.' He convinced me with his sincere compassion. I knew he would take care of me in any tight situation should it arise.

And so we made the trip on a very bumpy flight to Durban. We had met Kiki, Rodger, Minister Lyle and Vera for lunch before we went to the wedding, and they instantly fell in love with York, and all commented on how well I was looking in comparison to when I had left. It was certainly reassuring to hear.

As we placed our orders of orange juice and hamburgers, we all noticed a Hare Krishna man walking by, and we could not help but notice him with his bright orange robe and bald head except for a strip of yellow hair down the center. But what really grabbed our attention was what came hopping along behind him. An Indian minor bird was hopping in time with his steps, and it too was bald, and with its yellow beak, it was almost a mirror image of the Hare Krishna fellow*. We all paused, looked that bit longer and then looked at each other. Had we just seen that? We all tried to look again and craned our necks as the fellow, and the bird had by now gone passed us.

'Did you...?' Vera had not even finished her sentence when we all burst out laughing.

The waitress brought our drinks to the table amid our hysteria. York was collapsing with laughter, and as always his contagious laughter made us laugh even more. We were rocking in our chairs, back and forth, crying with laughter, except Rodger – he was too fat to rock, but his tummy wobbled and wiggled like a jelly monster. I knew I was laughing. I could feel the grumbling inside of me, my stomach hurt so much I held onto it for dear life, and my mouth was wide open and yet there was no sound coming out, but I was laughing as hard as I had ever laughed in my life. I managed to open my eyes and noticed that everyone was in the same predicament. Kiki was stomping her feet on the ground trying to bring an end to her laughter.

Slowly we all found our voices and looked at each other but the simple, surreal image of what we had just seen set us off again. When the waitress brought the burgers and with all the other patrons wondering what on earth was going on with us, we fought for self-control.

I tried to take a sip of my juice but landed up blowing bubbles as the giggles erupted, and that set me off again. By the time we were able actually to eat, our burgers were cold.

I wouldn't have traded that experience for anyone other than the wonderful people at that table at that moment. It was hardly possible to talk about anything else for the rest of our lunch date.

---

*My precious friend Kim and I witnessed this one day in Durban Central Park in 1980. It is still one of the most hilarious sights I have ever seen.

It had set the tone for what was going to be one of the most enjoyable weekends I'd had in years.

Rosalie's wedding was beautiful, she was beautiful, and I was grateful York had been convinced me to attend. A lot of our old friends were also there and that I got to see them made the trip all the more worthwhile.

We sat on the warm sand at Baggies early on Sunday morning. I felt at peace. York was right. I would be able to move forward from here. I had to let go of the past. I had to trust that God had a better plan for me.

From the beach, we went back to his aunt's house and bid our farewells and went to church. I was hesitant and anxious, even though Minister Lyle and Vera had assured me a hundred times at lunch that Spencer and Evelyn would not be there. That gnawing feeling clawed at my nerves until we were attending the Lord's Table and I gave my inhibitions to God and shared in His body and His blood. It was fantastic to visit with my old friends, but sadly we were not able to stay very long after service, as we had to catch our flight home.

Once a month instead of Bible study we had a 'share' meeting. My emotions seemed to have been all over the place since returning from the wedding. I wanted to remain angry with my enemies Spencer and Evelyn, and yet at the same time, I wanted to be happy. Something strange was going on inside of my heart. There was a joy that wanted to explode, and I did not know where it was coming from and why.

Most of the group seemed to have something to share that evening. When I was the last one left, I hesitated to mention my fears. I had avoided it at every share group so far. I opened my mouth to confess my fears, but nothing came out. The words eluded me; they simply banished themselves within the confines of my brain, to rather confuse me than to help me. I relented and offered nothing once more. I was disappointed in myself.

On our way home in York's comfortable car, he kept looking at me.

'What is it that stops you from sharing?' he finally asked as we waited at a red traffic light.

'If I speak about it I become angry, and the pain comes to the surface all over again, so it's best if it just gets left unsaid.'

He pulled off again as the lights changed.

'I think you are wrong. If you speak about it, it won't eat you up inside.'

I looked ahead of me not replying or looking his way.

'Hey chicky, I'm not forcing you into anything, I'm just saying it helps to get it off your chest.'

He rubbed my leg and smiled caringly. My heart leaped into another dimension.

He parked the car in the visitors' parking section, and we made our way to my apartment. Once inside I took off my thick red sweater, kicked off my sneakers, and walked around in my socks.

York stood by the kitchen nook and not wanting to let the subject drop he said, 'Okay, so tell me one thing, you don't want to forgive Spencer or Evelyn because if you do, then they get away with hurting you? Am I close?'

'You study psychology?' I asked avoiding his eyes.

'You know I haven't. Okay, so let me ask you this then. Are you perfect?'

'You know I'm not. No one is perfect.'

'Did Jesus die for you?'

'Yes,' I replied hesitantly, not sure where he was going with this.

'Did Jesus forgive you for your sins when he died for you?'

I stared at York, my eyes wide open as the realization finally sank in of what he just said.

'Jesus forgave me, so what am I if I cannot forgive them?'

York smiled at me, took two steps toward me and kissed me on the cheek.

'Now you got it chicky. Pray about it. How can you expect God to improve your life if you cannot forgive others? They have to atone for their sins one day. See you tomorrow.' Then he left, leaving me questioning my feelings.

Forgive them as I have forgiven you.

Those words rumbled through all rational reasoning and forced me to kneel beside my bed and pray and pray and pray until I had released the hurt and pain I had been harboring toward Spencer and Evelyn.

'Forgive them,' I finally asked, 'forgive me please Lord,' I begged.

I felt the weight on my shoulders get lighter, and I knew in my heart that the first step toward living a happy new life had begun.

Chapter Thirty-Six

Li was having a birthday party for her eldest son, and the first person he wanted to invite was York. No real surprise there. The party was very loud with thirty kids on a sugar high, running around screaming, yelling, jumping and even crying. York naturally entertained them almost the entire party.

'You should change your profession to being a party clown,' I said when York had escaped them for a few minutes, and we sat on the deck chairs in the backyard with the other adults. Lunch was a dose of hotdogs or boerewors rolls, and after hours of being one of the kids, York was famished. He ate several of both, scoffing them down in a hurry, probably worried the kids would fetch him, and he would not have enough time to eat his fill.

He laughed, 'I will take your suggestion seriously when my workshop folds. If that ever happens.'

When the last of the birthday guests had finally left, York sat outside enjoying the peace with Li's husband, and I helped Li clean up. What a mess there was everywhere, from the backyard all the way to the front gate.

'Note to self, never have children's parties at home,' I said aloud.

Li packed up laughing while filling up another black garbage bag of paper plates, cups, and party hats. After a cup of delicious coffee York and I left.

Once we were in the car York asked, 'You feel like going to the beach?'

'Aren't you exhausted? I thought you would want to crash and sleep the minute you left.'

'Nah, the weather is too good to be indoors, and there's still plenty of time before the sun sets.'

'The beach it is then,' I smiled happily.

I let the window of the car down and tilted my head so that the wind swept over my face, blowing the cool sea air onto me.

'You look much happier these days,' York said looking at me before pulling the car into the parking lot on Gordon's Bay beachfront.

I told him about my prayer and how I was finally able to forgive and move on. York had a smile as wide as a river.

'Told you. God works in amazing ways.'

He pushed his chest out smugly.

We bought ice-creams and walked along the beach. The sand was cool between my toes as they sunk in with each step, my body tingling with pleasure. I avoided the cold water.

York put his arm around my shoulders, our ice-creams consumed, and we continued to walk at a slow pace in time with the setting sun. The smell of the sea teased our senses; the tide was low exposing the rocks that were normally hidden during high tide. The sky blazed with bright orange and red stripes, too exquisite to paint. We stood and watched the sun sink below the horizon.

I rested my head on York's chest, his arm tightened around my shoulders, and ever so gently he kissed me on top of my head. With my arm wrapped around his waist, we were joined tightly together, my heart beating peacefully in time with his.

York moved so that we were facing each other, our noses almost touching, and I saw a determined look in his eyes as mine locked with his. We didn't say a word; our eyes did all the talking. He slowly leaned forward, and I allowed his lips to meet mine. A soft, gentle kiss at first and then he pulled away slightly waiting for my reaction. Would I run or not? I moved closer, my hand holding the side of his face encouraged him to kiss me again, and he obliged.

My toes curled deep into the sand, and my knees buckled so that I had to hold on to him to be able to stand up. I felt my heart collide with the stars. I thought I had been kissed before, but this kiss was beyond the force of the universe. My heart did a flick-flack then flipped, did a somersault and burst into a hop and a skip and then jumped against my ribcage, subsiding into a flutter of murmuring little wings.

When York finally withdrew, I gasped to get my breath back. I had no idea what to say to him. Whatever I did say would never do that kiss any justice.

He held me in his arms and softly said, 'I've waited forever to kiss you chicky.'

'You never said anything!' I squeaked out, still battling to get my racing heart back on track.

'I was always second in the line…'

'I'm so sorry; I was so stupid…'

He stilled my words with another kiss that awoke that joy in my heart that was waiting for a reason to explode. It burst into another galaxy. I wrapped my arms around his neck and pulled him closer to me so he could never leave and never be second again.

I was so in lost this earthly realm, engulfed by love, and I imagined God saying to me, 'So you finally made it to where I wanted you to be.'

Postscript

Unforgiveness is a killer! You cannot truly serve God if there is unforgiveness in your heart.

What does it help you if you live with bitterness and resentment toward someone?

You are the only one who suffers.

You cannot have a heart filled with happiness and at the same time have that same heart filled with unforgiveness.

When you truly forgive, your heart will find a joy indescribable.

God will carry your burdens, and He will admonish and pass judgment on your adversaries.

God forgave you, so who are you not to forgive others?

Ephesians 4:32   *"Be kind and compassionate to one another, forgiving each other, just as in Christ God forgave you."*

Your Opinion

You've come to the end of this story; I truly hope you enjoyed it and it touched your heart.

Please be kind and leave your review for the benefit of the many to follow, I will be so appreciative.

https://www.amazon.com/Second-Best-Aileen-Friedman-ebook/dp/B00IWS22EY/

Thank you
God bless you

Aileen Friedman

More Books By The Author

Aileen Friedman

Changes From a Sunset
ISBN 978-0-620-52564-0

When is My Forever
ISBN 978-0-620-55793-1

The Sparkle in Her Eyes plus Six more Short Stories
ISBN 978-0-620-64434-1

The day God came to earth.
ISBN 978-0-620-68628-0

Radar Love
ISBN 978-1-543-29950-2

Mr. Trolley Adventurer
ISBN 978-1-533-27328-4

Jamie's Discoveries
ISBN 978-1-533-27339-0

The Secret of Grace
ISBN 978-1-719-17242

www.ingramcontent.com/pod-product-compliance
Lightning Source LLC
Chambersburg PA
CBHW070923130626
46555CB00001B/254